PENGUIN BOOKS

RAISE HIGH THE ROOF BEAM, CARPENTERS *and* SEYMOUR – AN INTRODUCTION

J. D. SALINGER

RAISE HIGH THE ROOF BEAM, CARPENTERS

and

SEYMOUR–AN INTRODUCTION

PENGUIN BOOKS

PENGUIN BOOKS

Published by the Penguin Group
Penguin Books Ltd, 80 Strand, London WC2R ORL, England
Penguin Group (USA) Inc., 375 Hudson Street, New York, New York 10014, USA
Penguin Group (Canada), 90 Eglinton Avenue East, Suite 700, Toronto, Ontario, Canada M4P 2Y3
(a division of Pearson Penguin Canada Inc.)
Penguin Ireland, 25 St Stephen's Green, Dublin 2, Ireland (a division of Penguin Books Ltd)
Penguin Group (Australia), 250 Camberwell Road,
Camberwell, Victoria 3124, Australia (a division of Pearson Australia Group Pty Ltd)
Penguin Books India Pvt Ltd, 11 Community Centre, Panchsheel Park, New Delhi – 110 017, India
Penguin Group (NZ), 67 Apollo Drive, Rosedale, North Shore 0632, New Zealand
(a division of Pearson New Zealand Ltd)
Penguin Books (South Africa) (Pty) Ltd, 24 Sturdee Avenue, Rosebank, Johannesburg 2196, South Africa

Penguin Books Ltd, Registered Offices: 80 Strand, London WC2R ORL, England

www.penguin.com

'Raise High the Roof Beam, Carpenters' first published in the *New Yorker* 1955
'Seymour – An Introduction' first published in the *New Yorker* 1959
First published together in book form in the USA by Little, Brown 1963
First British edition published by William Heinemann 1963
Published in Penguin Books 1964
This original American edition first published in Great Britain 1994
Reissued in this edition by Penguin Books 2010

007

Printed and bound in Great Britain by Clays Ltd, Elcograf S.p.A.

ISBN: 978-0-141-04924-3

www.greenpenguin.co.uk

MIX
Paper | Supporting responsible forestry
FSC www.fsc.org FSC® C018179

Penguin Books is committed to a sustainable
future for our business, our readers and our planet.
This book is made from Forest Stewardship
Council™ certified paper.

If there is an amateur reader still left in the world – or anybody who just reads and runs – I ask him or her, with untellable affection and gratitude, to split the dedication of this book four ways with my wife and children.

RAISE HIGH THE ROOF BEAM, CARPENTERS

One night some twenty years ago, during a siege of mumps in our enormous family, my youngest sister, Franny, was moved, crib and all, into the ostensibly germ-free room I shared with my eldest brother, Seymour. I was fifteen, Seymour was seventeen. Along about two in the morning, the new roommate's crying wakened me. I lay in a still, neutral position for a few minutes, listening to the racket, till I heard, or felt, Seymour stir in the bed next to mine. In those days, we kept a flashlight on the night table between us, for emergencies that, as far as I remember, never arose. Seymour turned it on and got out of bed. 'The bottle's on the stove, Mother said,' I told him. 'I gave it to her a little while ago,' Seymour said. 'She isn't hungry.' He went over in the dark to the bookcase and beamed the flashlight slowly back and forth along the stacks. I sat up in bed. 'What are you going to do?' I said. 'I thought maybe I'd read something to her,' Seymour said, and took down a book. 'She's ten months old, for God's sake,' I said. 'I know,' Seymour said. 'They have ears. They can hear.'

The story Seymour read to Franny that night, by flashlight, was a favorite of his, a Taoist tale. To this day, Franny swears that she remembers Seymour reading it to her:

> Duke Mu of Chin said to Po Lo: 'You are now advanced in years. Is there any member of your family whom I could employ to look for horses in your stead?' Po Lo replied: 'A good horse can be picked out by its general build and appearance. But the superlative horse – one that raises no dust and leaves no tracks – is something evanescent and fleeting, elusive as thin air. The talents of my sons lie on a lower plane altogether; they can tell a good horse when they see one, but they cannot tell a superlative horse. I have a friend, however, one Chiu-fang Kao, a hawker of fuel and vegetables, who in things appertaining to horses is nowise my inferior. Pray see him.'
>
> Duke Mu did so, and subsequently dispatched him on the quest for a steed. Three months later, he returned with the news that he had found one. 'It is now in Shach'iu,' he added. 'What kind of a horse is

it?' asked the Duke. 'Oh, it is a dun-colored mare,' was the reply. However, someone being sent to fetch it, the animal turned out to be a coal-black stallion! Much displeased, the Duke sent for Po Lo. 'That friend of yours,' he said, 'whom I commissioned to look for a horse, has made a fine mess of it. Why, he cannot even distinguish a beast's color or sex! What on earth can he know about horses?' Po Lo heaved a sigh of satisfaction. 'Has he really got as far as that?' he cried. 'Ah, then he is worth ten thousand of me put together. There is no comparison between us. What Kao keeps in view is the spiritual mechanism. In making sure of the essential, he forgets the homely details; intent on the inward qualities, he loses sight of the external. He sees what he wants to see, and not what he does not want to see. He looks at the things he ought to look at, and neglects those that need not be looked at. So clever a judge of horses is Kao, that he has it in him to judge something better than horses.'

When the horse arrived, it turned out indeed to be a superlative animal.

I've reproduced the tale here not just because I invariably go out of my way to recommend a good prose pacifier to parents or older brothers of ten-month-old babies but for quite another reason. What directly follows is an account of a wedding day in 1942. It is, in my opinion, a self-contained account, with a beginning and an end, and a mortality, all its own. Yet, because I'm in possession of the fact, I feel I must mention that the bridegroom is now, in 1955, no longer living. He committed suicide in 1948, while he was on vacation in Florida with his wife . . . Undoubtedly, though, what I'm really getting at is this: Since the bridegroom's permanent retirement from the scene, I haven't been able to think of anybody whom I'd care to send out to look for horses in his stead.

In late May of 1942, the progeny – seven in number – of Les and Bessie (Gallagher) Glass, retired Pantages Circuit vaudevillians, were flung, extravagantly speaking, all over the United States. I, for one, the second-eldest, was in the post hospital at Fort Benning, Georgia, with pleurisy – a little keepsake of thirteen weeks' infantry basic training. The twins, Walt and Waker, had been split up a whole year earlier. Waker was in a conscientious objectors' camp in Maryland, and Walt was somewhere in the Pacific – or on his way there – with a field-artillery unit. (We've never been altogether sure where Walt was at that specific time. He was never a great letter writer, and very little personal information – almost none – reached us after his death. He was killed in an unspeakably absurd G.I. accident in late autumn of 1945, in Japan.) My eldest sister, Boo Boo, who comes, chronologically, between the twins and me, was an ensign in the Waves, stationed, off and on, at a naval base in Brooklyn. All that spring and summer, she occupied the small apartment in New York that my brother Seymour and I had all but technically given up after our induction. The two youngest children in the family, Zooey (male) and Franny (female), were with our parents in Los Angeles, where my father was hustling talent for a motion-picture studio. Zooey was thirteen, and Franny was eight. They were both appearing every week on a children's radio quiz program called, with perhaps typically pungent Coast-to-Coast irony, 'It's a Wise Child.' At one time or another, I might well bring in here – or, rather, in one year or another – all the children in our family have been weekly hired 'guests' on 'It's a Wise Child.' Seymour and I were the first to appear on the show, back in 1927, at the respective ages of ten and eight, in the days when the program 'emanated' from one of the convention rooms of the old Murray Hill Hotel. All seven of us, from Seymour through Franny, appeared on the show under pseudonyms. Which may sound highly anomalous, considering that we're the children of vaudevillians, a sect not usually antipathetic to publicity, but my mother had once read a magazine article on the little crosses professional children are obliged to bear – their estrangement from normal, presumably desirable society – and she took an iron stand on the issue, and never, never wavered. (This is not the time at all to go into the question of whether most, or all, 'professional' children ought to be outlawed, pitied, or unsentimentally executed as disturbers of the peace. For the moment, I'll only pass along that our combined income on 'It's a Wise Child' has sent six of us through college, and is now sending the seventh.)

Our eldest brother, Seymour – with whom I'm all but

exclusively concerned here – was a corporal in what, in 1942, was still called the Air Corps. He was stationed at a B-17 base in California, where, I *believe*, he was an acting company clerk. I might add, not quite parenthetically, that he was by far the least prolific letter writer in the family. I don't think I've had five letters from him in my life.

On the morning of either May 22nd or 3rd (no one in my family has ever dated a letter), a letter from my sister Boo Boo was placed on the foot of my cot in the post hospital at Fort Benning while my diaphragm was being strapped with adhesive tape (a usual medical procedure with pleurisy patients, presumably guaranteed to prevent them from coughing themselves to pieces). When the ordeal was over, I read Boo Boo's letter. I still have it, and it follows here verbatim:

DEAR BUDDY,

I'm in a terrible rush to pack, so this will be short but *penetrating*. Admiral Behind-pincher has decided that he must fly to parts unknown for the war effort and has also decided to take his secretary with him if I behave myself. I'm just sick about it. Seymour aside, it means Quonset huts in freezing air bases and boyish passes from our fighting men and those horrible paper things to get sick in on the plane. The point is, Seymour is getting married – yes, *married*, so please pay attention. I can't be there. I may be gone for anywhere from six weeks to two months on this trip. I've met the girl. She's a zero in my opinion but terrific-looking. I don't actually *know* that she's a zero. I mean she hardly said two words the night I met her. Just sat and smiled and smoked, so it isn't fair to say. I don't know anything about the romance itself at all, except that they apparently met when Seymour was stationed at Monmouth last winter. The mother is the end – a finger in all the arts, and sees a good Jungian man twice a week (she asked me twice, the night I met her, if I'd ever been analyzed). She told me she just wishes Seymour would *relate* to more people. In the same breath, said she just loves him, though, etc., etc., and that she used to listen to him religiously all the years he was on the air. That's all I know except that you've *got* to get to the wedding. I'll never forgive you if you don't. I mean it. Mother and Daddy can't get here from the Coast. Franny has the measles, for one thing. Incidentally, did you hear her last week? She went on at beautiful length about how she used to fly all around the apartment when she was four and no one was home. The new announcer is worse than Grant – if possible, even worse than Sullivan in the old days. He said she surely just *dreamt* that she was able to fly. The baby stood her ground like an angel. She said she *knew* she was able to fly because when she came down she always had dust on her fingers from touching the light bulbs. I long to see her. You, too. Anyhow, you've *got* to get to the wedding. Go A.W.O.L. if you have to, but please *go*. It's at three o'clock, June 4th. *Very* non-sectarian and Emancipated, at her grandmother's house on 63rd. Some judge is marrying them. I don't know the number of the house, but it's exactly two doors down from where Carl and Amy used to live in luxury. I'm going to wire Walt, but I think he's been shipped out already. *Please* get there, Buddy. He weighs about as much as a cat and he has that ecstatic look on his face that you can't talk to. Maybe it's going to be perfectly all right, but I hate 1942. I think I'll hate 1942 till I die, just on general principles. All my love and see you when I get back.

BOO BOO

A couple of days after the letter arrived, I was discharged from the hospital, in the custody, so to speak, of about three yards of adhesive tape around my ribs. Then began a very strenuous week's campaign to get permission to attend the wedding. I was finally able to do it by laboriously ingratiating myself with my company commander, a bookish man by his own confession, whose favorite author, as luck had it, happened to be my favorite author – L. Manning Vines. Or Hinds. Despite this spiritual bond between us, the most I could wangle out of him was a three-day pass, which would, at best, give me just enough time to travel by train to New York, see the wedding, bolt a dinner somewhere, and then return damply to Georgia.

All sit-up coaches on trains in 1942 were only nominally ventilated, as I remember, abounded with M.P.s, and smelled of orange juice, milk, and rye whiskey. I spent the night coughing and reading a copy of Ace Comics that someone was kind enough to lend me. When the train pulled into New York – at ten after two on the afternoon of the wedding – I was coughed out, generally exhausted, perspiring, unpressed, and my adhesive tape was itching hellishly. New York itself was indescribably hot. I had no time to go to my apartment first, so I left my luggage, which consisted of a rather oppressive-looking little canvas zipper bag, in one of those steel boxes at Penn Station. To make things still more provocative, as I was wandering around in the garment district trying to find an empty cab, a second lieutenant in the Signal Corps, whom I'd apparently overlooked saluting, crossing Seventh Avenue, suddenly took out a fountain pen and wrote down my name, serial number, and address while a number of civilians looked interestedly on.

I was limp when I finally got into a cab. I gave the driver directions that would take me at least as far as 'Carl and Amy's' old house. As soon as we arrived in that block, however, it was very simple. One just followed the crowd. There was even a canvas canopy. A moment later, I entered an enormous old brownstone and was met by a very handsome, lavender-haired woman, who asked me whether I was a friend of the bride or the groom. I said the groom. 'Oh,' she said, 'well, we're just bunching everybody up together.' She laughed rather immoderately, and showed me to what seemed to be the last vacant folding chair in a very crowded outsize room. I have a thirteen-year-old blackout in my mind with regard to the over-all physical details of the room. Beyond the fact that it was jam-packed and stifling hot, I can remember only two things: that there was an organ playing almost directly behind me, and that the woman in the seat directly at my right turned to me and enthusiastically stage-whispered, '*I'm Helen Silsburn!*' From the location of our seats, I gathered that she was not the bride's mother, but, to play it safe, I smiled and nodded gregariously, and was about to say who *I* was, but she put a decorous finger to her lips, and we both faced front. It was then, roughly, three o'clock. I closed my eyes and waited, a trifle guardedly, for the organist to quit the incidental music and plunge into 'Lohengrin.'

I haven't a very clear idea of how the next hour and a quarter passed, aside from the cardinal fact that there was no plunging into 'Lohengrin.' I remember a little dispersed band of unfamiliar faces that surreptitiously turned around, now and then, to see who was coughing. And I remember that the woman at my right addressed me once again, in the same rather festive whisper.

'There must be some delay,' she said. 'Have you ever seen Judge Ranker? He has the face of a *saint*.' And I remember the organ music veering peculiarly, almost desperately, at one point, from Bach to early Rodgers and Hart. On the whole, though, I'm afraid, I passed the time paying little sympathetic hospital calls on myself for being obliged to suppress my coughing spells. I had a sustained, cowardly notion, the entire time I was in the room, that I was about to hemorrhage, or, at the very least, fracture a rib, despite the corset of adhesive tape I was wearing.

At twenty minutes past four – or, to put it another, blunter way, an hour and twenty minutes past what seemed to be all reasonable hope – the unmarried bride, her head down, a parent stationed on either side of her, was helped out of the building and conducted, fragilely, down a long flight of stone steps to the sidewalk. She was then deposited – almost hand over hand, it seemed – into the first of the sleek black hired cars that were waiting, double-parked, at the curb. It was an excessively graphic moment – a tabloid moment – and, as tabloid moments go, it had its full complement of eyewitnesses, for the wedding guests (myself among them) had already begun to pour out of the building, however decorously, in alert, not to say goggle-eyed, droves. If there was any even faintly lenitive aspect to the spectacle, the weather itself was responsible for it. The June sun was so hot and so glaring, of such multi-flashbulb-like mediacy, that the image of the bride, as she made her almost invalided way down the stone steps, tended to blur where blurring mattered most.

Once the bridal car was at least physically removed from the scene, the tension on the sidewalk – especially around the mouth of the canvas canopy, at the curb, where I, for one, was loitering – deteriorated into what, had the building been a church, and had it been a Sunday, might have been taken for fairly normal congregation-dispersing confusion. Then, very suddenly, the emphasized word came – reportedly from the bride's Uncle Al – that the wedding guests were to *use* the cars standing at the curb; that is, reception or no reception, change of plans or no change of plans. If the reaction in my vicinity was any criterion, the offer was generally received as a kind of *beau geste*. It didn't quite go without saying, however, that the cars were to be 'used' only after a formidable-looking platoon of people – referred to as the bride's 'immediate family' – had taken what transportation *they* needed to quit the scene. And, after a somewhat mysterious and bottleneck-like delay (during which I remained peculiarly riveted to the spot), the 'immediate family' did indeed begin to make its exodus, as many as six or seven persons to a car, or as few as three or four. The number, I gathered, depended upon the age, demeanor, and hip spread of the first occupants in possession.

Suddenly, at someone's parting – but markedly crisp – suggestion, I found myself stationed at the curb, directly at the mouth of the canvas canopy, attending to helping people into cars.

How I had been singled out to fill this post deserves some small speculation. So far as I know, the unidentified, middle-aged man of action who had picked me for the job hadn't a glimmer of a notion that I was the bridegroom's brother. Therefore, it seems logical that I was singled out for other, far less poetic reasons. The year was 1942. I was twenty-three, and newly drafted into the Army. It strikes me that it was solely my age, my uniform, and the unmistakably serviceable, olive-drab aura about me that had left no doubt concerning my eligibility to fill in as doorman.

I was not only twenty-three but a conspicuously retarded twenty-three. I remember loading people into cars without any degree of competence whatever. On the contrary, I went about it with a certain disingenuous, cadetlike semblance of single-mindedness, of adherence to duty. After a few minutes, in fact, I became all too aware that I was catering to the needs of a predominantly older, shorter, fleshier generation, and my performance as an arm taker and door closer took on an even more thoroughly bogus puissance. I began to conduct myself like an exceptionally adroit, wholly engaging young giant with a cough.

But the heat of the afternoon was, to say the least, oppressive, and the compensations of my office must have seemed to me increasingly tokenless. Abruptly, though the crowd of 'immediate family' seemed scarcely to have begun to thin out, I myself lunged into one of the freshly loaded cars, just as it started to draw away from the curb. In doing it, I hit my head a very audible (perhaps retributive) crack on the roof. One of the occupants of the car was none other than my whispering acquaintance, Helen Silsburn, and she started to offer me her unqualified sympathy. The crack had evidently resounded throughout the car. But at twenty-three I was the sort of young man who responds to all public injury of his person, short of a fractured skull, by giving out a hollow, subnormal-sounding laugh.

The car moved west, directly, as it were, into the open furnace of the late-afternoon sky. It continued west for two blocks, till it reached Madison Avenue, and then it right-angled sharply north. I felt as though we were all being saved from being caught up by the sun's terrible flue only by the anonymous driver's enormous alertness and skill.

The first four or five blocks north on Madison, conversation in the car was chiefly limited to remarks like 'Am I giving you enough room?' and 'I've never been so *hot* in my entire life.' The one who had never been so hot in her entire life was, as I'd learned from a certain amount of eavesdropping at the curb, the bride's Matron of Honor. She was a hefty girl of about twenty-four or -five, in a pink satin dress, with a circlet of artificial forget-me-nots in her hair. There was a distinctly athletic ethos about her, as if, a year or two earlier, she might have majored in physical education in college. In her lap she was holding a bouquet of gardenias rather as though it were a deflated volleyball. She was seated in the back of the car, hip-pressed between her husband and a tiny elderly man in a top hat and cutaway, who was holding an unlighted clear-Havana cigar. Mrs Silsburn and I – our respective inside knees unribaldly touching – occupied the jump seats. Twice, without any excuse whatever, out of sheer approval, I glanced around at the tiny elderly man. When I'd originally loaded the car and held the door open for him, I'd had a passing impulse to pick him up bodily and insert him gently through the open window. He was tininess itself, surely being not more than four nine or ten and without being either a midget or a dwarf. In the car, he sat staring very severely straight ahead of him. On my second look around at him, I noticed that he had what very much appeared to be an old gravy stain on the lapel of his cutaway. I also noticed that his silk hat cleared the roof of the car by a good four or five inches . . . But for the most part, those first few minutes in the car, I was still mainly concerned with my own state of health. Besides having pleurisy and a bruised head, I had a hypochondriac's notion that I was getting a strep throat. I sat surreptitiously curling back my tongue and exploring the suspected ailing part. I was staring, as I remember, directly in front of me, at the back of the driver's neck, which was a relief map of boil scars, when suddenly my jump-seat mate addressed me: 'I didn't get a chance to ask you inside. How's that darling mother of yours? Aren't you Dickie Briganza?'

My tongue, at the time of the question, was curled back exploratively as far as the soft palate. I disentangled it, swallowed, and turned to her. She was fifty, or thereabouts, fashionably and tastefully dressed. She was wearing a very heavy pancake makeup. I answered no – that I wasn't.

She narrowed her eyes a trifle at me and said I looked exactly like Celia Briganza's boy. Around the mouth. I tried to show by my expression that it was a mistake anybody could make. Then I went on staring at the back of the driver's neck. The car was silent. I glanced out of the window, for a change of scene.

'How do you like the Army?' Mrs Silsburn asked. Abruptly, conversationally.

I had a brief coughing spell at that particular instant. When it was over, I turned to her with all available alacrity and said I'd made a lot of buddies. It was a little difficult for me to swivel in her direction, what with the encasement of adhesive tape around my diaphragm.

She nodded. 'I think you're all just wonderful,' she said, somewhat ambiguously. 'Are you a friend of the bride's or the groom's?' she then asked, delicately getting down to brass tacks.

'Well, actually, I'm not exactly a friend of –'

"You'd better not say you're a friend of the *groom*,' the Matron of Honor interrupted me, from the back of the car. 'I'd like to get my hands on him for about *two minutes*. Just *two minutes*, that's all.'

Mrs Silsburn turned briefly – but completely – around to smile at the speaker. Then she faced front again. We made the round trip, in fact, almost in unison. Considering that Mrs Silsburn had turned around for only an instant, the smile she had bestowed on the Matron of Honor was a kind of jump-seat masterpiece. It was vivid enough to express unlimited partisanship with all young people, all over the world, but most particularly with this spirited, outspoken local representative, to whom, perhaps, she had been little more than perfunctorily introduced, if at all.

'Bloodthirsty wench,' said a chuckling male voice. And Mrs Silsburn and I turned around again. It was the Matron of Honor's husband who had spoken up. He was seated directly behind me, at his wife's left. He and I briefly exchanged that blank, uncomradely look which, possibly, in the crapulous year of 1942, only an officer and a private could exchange. A first lieutenant in the Signal Corps, he was wearing a very interesting Air Corps pilot's cap – a visored hat with the metal frame removed from inside the crown, which usually conferred on the wearer a certain, presumably desired, intrepid look. In his case, however, the cap didn't begin to fill the bill. It seemed to serve no other purpose than to make my own outsize, regulation headpiece feel rather like a clown's hat that someone had nervously picked out of the incinerator. His face was sallow and, essentially, daunted-looking. He was perspiring with an almost incredible profusion – on his forehead, on his upper lip, and even at the end of his nose – to the point where a salt tablet might have been in order. 'I'm married to the bloodthirstiest wench in six counties,' he said, addressing Mrs Silsburn and giving another soft, public chuckle. In automatic deference to his rank, I very nearly chuckled right along with him – a short, inane, stranger's and draftee's chuckle that would clearly signify that I was with him and everyone else in the car, against no one.

'I *mean* it,' the Matron of Honor said. 'Just two minutes – that's all, brother. Oh, if I could just get my two little *hands* –'

'All right, now, take it easy, take it easy,' her husband said, still with apparently inexhaustible resources of connubial good humor. 'Just take it easy. You'll last longer.'

Mrs Silsburn faced around toward the back of the car again, and favored the Matron of Honor with an all but canonized smile. 'Did anyone see any of his people at the wedding?' she inquired softly, with just a little emphasis – no more than perfectly genteel – on the personal pronoun.

The Matron of Honor's answer came with toxic volume: '*No*. They're all out on the West *Coast* or someplace. I just wish I *had*.'

Her husband's chuckle sounded again. 'What wouldja done if you had, honey?' he asked – and winked indiscriminately at me.

'Well, I don't *know*, but I'd've done *some*thing,' said the Matron of Honor. The chuckle at her left expanded in volume. 'Well, I would have!' she insisted. 'I'd've said *some*thing to them. I mean. My gosh.' She spoke with increasing aplomb, as though perceiving that, cued by her husband, the rest of us within earshot were finding something attractively forthright – spunky – about her sense of justice, however youthful or impractical it might be. 'I don't know *what* I'd have said to them. I probably would have just blabbered something idiotic. But my *gosh*. Honestly! I just can't stand to see somebody get away with absolute murder. It makes my blood boil.' She suspended animation just long enough to be bolstered by a look of simulated empathy from Mrs Silsburn. Mrs Silsburn and I were now turned completely, supersociably, around in our jump seats. 'I *mean* it,' the Matron of Honor said. 'You can't just *barge* through life hurting people's feelings whenever you feel like it.'

'I'm afraid I know very little about the young man,' Mrs Silsburn said, softly. 'As a matter of fact, I haven't even met him. The first I'd heard that Muriel was even engaged –'

'*Nobody's* met him,' the Matron of Honor said, rather explosively. '*I* haven't even met him. We had two rehearsals, and both times Muriel's poor father had to take his place, just because his crazy plane couldn't take off. He was supposed to get a hop here last Tuesday night in some crazy Army plane, but it was *snowing* or something crazy in Colorado, or Ari*zona*, or one of those crazy places, and he didn't get in till one o'clock in the *morning, last night. Then* – at that insane hour – he calls Muriel on the phone from way out in Long *Island* or someplace and asks her to meet him in the lobby of some horrible hotel so they can *talk*.' The Matron of Honor shuddered eloquently. 'And you know Muriel. She's just darling enough to let anybody and his brother push her around. That's what gripes me. It's always those kind of people that get hurt in the end . . . Anyway, so she gets dressed and gets in a cab and sits in some horrible lobby talking with him till quarter to *five* in the morning.' The Matron of Honor released her grip on her gardenia bouquet long enough to raise two clenched fists above her lap. '*Ooo*, it makes me so mad!' she said.

'What hotel?' I asked the Matron of Honor. 'Do you know?' I tried to make my voice sound casual, as though, possibly, my father might be in the hotel business and I took a certain understandable filial interest in where people stopped in New York. In reality, my question meant almost nothing. I was just thinking aloud, more or less. I'd been interested in the fact that my brother had asked his fiancée to meet him in a hotel lobby, rather than at his empty, available apartment. The morality of the invitation was by no means out of character, but it interested me, mildly, nonetheless.

'*I* don't know which hotel,' the Matron of Honor said irritably. 'Just some ho*tel*.' She stared at me. 'Why?' she demanded. 'Are you a friend of his?'

There was something distinctly intimidating about her stare. It seemed to come from a one-woman mob, separated only by time and chance from her knitting bag and a splendid view of the guillotine. I've been terrified of mobs, of any kind, all my life. 'We were boys together,' I answered, all but unintelligibly.

'Well, lucky you!'

'Now, now,' said her husband.

'Well, I'm *sorry*,' the Matron of Honor said to him, but addressing all of us. 'But you haven't been in a room watching that poor kid cry her eyes out for a solid hour. It's not funny – and don't you forget it. I've heard about grooms getting cold feet, and all that. But you don't do it at the *last minute*. I mean you don't do it so that you'll embarrass a lot of perfectly nice people half to death and almost break a kid's spirit and everything! If he'd changed his *mind*, why didn't he write to her and at least break it off like a gentleman, for goodness' sake? Before all the damage was done.'

'All right, take it easy, just take it easy,' her husband said. His chuckle was still there, but it was sounding a trifle strained.

'Well, I mean it! Why couldn't he write to her and just tell her, like a *man*, and prevent all this tragedy and everything?' She looked at me, abruptly. 'Do you have any idea where he is, by any chance?' she demanded, with metal in her voice. 'If you were *boyhood* friends, you should have some –'

'I just got into New York about two hours ago,' I said nervously. Not only the Matron of Honor but her husband and Mrs Silsburn as well were now staring at me. 'So far, I haven't even had a chance to get to a phone.' At that point, as I remember, I had a coughing spell. It was genuine enough, but I must say I did very little to suppress it or shorten its duration.

'You had that cough looked at, soldier?' the Lieutenant asked me when I'd come out of it.

At that instant, I had another coughing spell – a perfectly genuine one, oddly enough. I was still turned a sort of half or quarter right in my jump seat, with my body averted just enough toward the front of the car to be able to cough with all due hygienic propriety.

It seems very disorderly, but I think a paragraph ought to be wedged in right here to answer a couple of stumpers. First off, why did I go on sitting in the car? Aside from all incidental considerations, the car was reportedly destined to deliver its occupants to the bride's parents' apartment house. No amount of information, first- or secondhand, that I might have acquired from the prostrate, unmarried bride or from her disturbed (and, very likely, angry) parents could possibly have made up for the awkwardness of my presence in their apartment. Why, then, did I go on sitting in the car? Why didn't I get out while, say, we were stopped for a red light? And, still more salient, why had I jumped into the car in the first place? . . . There seem to me at least a dozen answers to these questions, and all of them, however dimly, valid enough. I think, though, that I can dispense with them, and just reiterate that the year was 1942, that I was twenty-three, newly drafted, newly advised in the efficacy of keeping close to the herd – and, above all, I felt lonely. One simply jumped into loaded cars, as I see it, and stayed seated in them.

To get back to the plot, I remember that while all three – the Matron of Honor, her husband, and Mrs Silsburn – were conjunctively staring at me and watching me cough, I glanced over at the tiny elderly man in the back. He was still staring fixedly straight ahead of him. I noticed, almost with gratitude, that his feet didn't quite touch the floor. They looked like old and valued friends of mine.

'What's this man supposed to *do*, anyway?' the Matron of Honor said to me when I'd emerged from my second coughing spell.

'You mean Seymour?' I said. It seemed clear, at first, from her inflection, that she had something singularly ignominious in mind. Then, suddenly, it struck me – and it was sheerly intuitive – that she might well be in secret possession of a motley number of biographical facts about Seymour; that is, the low, regrettably dramatic, and (in my opinion) basically misleading facts about him. That he'd been Billy Black, a national radio 'celebrity,' for some six years of his boyhood. Or that, for another example, he'd been a freshman at Columbia when he'd just turned fifteen.

'Yes, *Sey*mour,' said the Matron of Honor. 'What'd he do before he was in the Army?'

Again I had the same little effulgent flash of intuition that she knew much more about him than, for some reason, she meant to indicate. It seemed, for one thing, that she knew perfectly well that Seymour had been teaching English before his induction – that he'd been a professor. A *professor*. For an instant, in fact, as I looked at her, I had a very uncomfortable notion that she might even know that I was Seymour's brother. It wasn't a thought to dwell on. Instead, I looked her unsquarely in the eye and said, 'He was a chiropodist.' Then, abruptly, I faced around and looked out of my window. The car had been motionless for some minutes, and I had just become aware of the sound of martial drums in the distance, from the general direction of Lexington or Third Avenue.

'It's a parade!' said Mrs Silsburn. She had faced around, too.

We were in the upper Eighties. A policeman was stationed in the middle of Madison Avenue and was halting all north- and south-bound traffic. So far as I could tell, he was *just* halting it; that is, not redirecting it either east or west. There were three or four cars and a bus waiting to move southward, but our car chanced to be the only vehicle aimed uptown. At the immediate corner, and at what I could see of the uptown side street leading toward Fifth Avenue, people were standing two and three deep along the curb and on the walk, waiting, apparently, for a detail of troops, or nurses, or Boy Scouts, or what-have-you, to leave their assembly point at Lexington or Third Avenue and march past.

'Oh, *Lord*. Wouldn't you just know?' said the Matron of Honor.

I turned around and very nearly bumped heads with her. She was leaning forward, toward and all but into the space between Mrs Silsburn and me. Mrs Silsburn turned toward her, too, with a responsive, rather pained expression.

'We may be here for *weeks*,' the Matron of Honor said, craning forward to see out of the driver's windshield. 'I should be there *now*. I told Muriel and her mother I'd be in one of the first cars and that I'd get up to the house in about *five minutes*. Oh, God! Can't we *do* something?'

'I should be there, too,' Mrs Silsburn said, rather promptly.

'Yes, but I solemnly *promised* her. The apartment's gonna be loaded with all kinds of crazy aunts and uncles and absolute strangers, and I told her I'd stand *guard* with about ten bayonets and see that she got a little privacy and –' She broke off. 'Oh, God. This is awful.'

Mrs Silsburn gave a small, stilted laugh. 'I'm afraid I'm one of the crazy aunts,' she said. Clearly, she was affronted.

The Matron of Honor looked at her. 'Oh – I'm sorry. I didn't mean you,' she said. She sat back in her seat. 'I just meant that their apartment's so tiny, and if everybody starts pouring in by the dozens – You know what I mean.'

Mrs Silsburn said nothing, and I didn't look at her to see just how seriously she'd been affronted by the Matron of Honor's remark. I remember, though, that I was impressed, in a peculiar sense, with the Matron of Honor's tone of apology for her little slip about 'crazy aunts and uncles.' It had been a genuine apology, but not an embarrassed and, still better, not an obsequious one, and for a moment I had a feeling that, for all her stagy indignation and showy grit, there *was* something bayonetlike about her, something not altogether unadmirable. (I'll grant, quickly and readily, that my opinion in this instance has a very limited value. I often feel a rather excessive pull toward people who don't over-apologize.) The point is, however, that right then, for the first time, a small wave of prejudice against the missing groom passed over me, a just perceptible little whitecap of censure for his unexplained absenteeism.

'Let's see if we can get a little action around here,' the Matron of Honor's husband said. It was rather the voice of a man who keeps calm under fire. I felt him deploying behind me, and then, abruptly, his head craned into the limited space between Mrs Silsburn and me. 'Driver,' he said peremptorily, and waited for a response. When it came with promptness, his voice became a bit more tractile, democratic: 'How long do you think we'll be tied up here?'

The driver turned around. 'You got me, Mac,' he said. He faced front again. He was absorbed in what was going on at the intersection. A minute earlier, a small boy with a partly deflated red balloon had run out into the cleared, forbidden street. He had just been captured and was being dragged back to the curb by his father, who gave the boy two only partly openhanded punches between the shoulder blades. The act was righteously booed by the crowd.

'Did you *see* what that man did to that *child*?' Mrs Silsburn demanded of everyone in general. No one answered her.

'What about asking that cop how long we're apt to be held up here?' the Matron of Honor's husband said to the driver. He was still leaning forward. He'd evidently not been altogether satisfied with the laconic reply to his first question. 'We're all in something of a hurry, you know. Do you think you could ask him how long we're apt to be tied up here?'

Without turning around, the driver rudely shrugged his shoulders. But he turned off his ignition, and got out of the car, slamming the heavy limousine door behind him. He was an untidy, bullish-looking man in partial chauffeur's livery – a black serge suit, but no cap.

He walked slowly and very independently, not to say insolently, the few steps over to the intersection, where the ranking policeman was directing things. The two then stood talking to each other for an endless amount of time. (I heard the Matron of Honor give a groan, behind me.) Then, suddenly, the two men broke into uproarious laughter – as though they hadn't really been conversing at all but had been exchanging very short dirty jokes. Then our driver, still laughing uninfectiously, waved a fraternal hand at the cop and walked – slowly – back to the car. He got in, slammed his door shut, extracted a cigarette from a package on the ledge over the dashboard, tucked the cigarette behind his ear, and then, and then only, turned around to make his report to us. 'He don't know,' he said. 'We gotta wait for the parade to pass by here.' He gave us, collectively, an indifferent once-over. 'After that we can go ahead O.K.' He faced front, disengaged the cigarette from behind his ear, and lit it.

In the back of the car, the Matron of Honor sounded a voluminous little plaint of frustration and pique. And then there was silence. For the first time in several minutes, I glanced around at the tiny elderly man with the unlighted cigar. The delay didn't seem to affect him. His standard of comportment for sitting in the rear seat of cars – cars in motion, cars stationary, and even, one couldn't help imagining, cars that were driven off bridges into rivers – seemed to be fixed. It was wonderfully simple. You just sat very erect, maintaining a clearance of four or five inches between your top hat and the roof, and you stared ferociously ahead at the windshield. If Death – who was out there all the time, possibly sitting on the hood – if Death stepped miraculously through the glass and came in after you, in all probability you just got up and went along with him, ferociously but quietly. Chances were, you could take your cigar with you, if it was a clear Havana.

'What are we going to do? Just *sit* here?' the Matron of Honor said. 'I'm so hot I could die.' And Mrs Silsburn and I turned around just in time to see her look at her husband directly for the first time since they'd got into the car. 'Can't you move over just a tiny little bit?' she said to him. 'I'm so squashed in here I can hardly breathe.'

The Lieutenant, chuckling, opened his hands expressively. 'I'm practically sitting on the fender now, Bunny,' he said.

The Matron of Honor then looked over, with mixed curiosity and disapproval, at her other seatmate, who, as though unconsciously dedicated to cheering me up, was occupying far more space than he needed. There was a good two inches between his right hip and the base of the outside armrest. The Matron of Honor undoubtedly noticed it, too, but, for all her metal, she didn't quite have what it would have taken to speak up to that formidable-looking little personage. She turned back to her husband. 'Can you reach your cigarettes?' she said irritably. 'I'll never get mine out, the way we're packed in here.' With the words 'packed in,' she turned her head again to shoot a brief, all-implicit look at the tiny guilty party who had usurped the space she thought ought rightfully to be hers. He remained sublimely out of touch. He went on glaring straight ahead of him, toward the driver's windshield. The Matron of Honor looked at Mrs Silsburn, and raised her eyebrows expressively. Mrs Silsburn responded with a countenance full of understanding and sympathy. The Lieutenant, meanwhile, had shifted his weight over to his left, or window-side, buttock, and from the right-hand pocket of his officer's pinks had taken out a package of cigarettes and a folder of matches. His wife picked out a cigarette, and waited for a light, which was immediately forthcoming. Mrs Silsburn and I watched the lighting of the cigarette as though it were a moderately bewitching novelty.

'Oh, pardon *me*,' the Lieutenant suddenly said, and extended his cigarette pack to Mrs Silsburn.

'No, thank you. I don't smoke,' Mrs Silsburn said quickly – almost with regret.

'Soldier?' the Lieutenant said, extending the pack to me, after the most imperceptible of hesitations. In all truth, I rather liked him for putting through the offer, for the small victory of common courtesy over caste, but I declined the cigarette.

'May I see your matches?' Mrs Silsburn said, in an exceedingly diffident, almost little-girlish voice.

'These?' said the Lieutenant. He handed his folder of matches readily over to Mrs Silsburn.

While I looked on with an expression of absorption, Mrs Silsburn examined the match folder. On its outside cover, in gold letters on a crimson background, were printed the words 'These Matches Were Stolen from Bob and Edie Burwick's House.' '*Dar*ling,' Mrs Silsburn said, shaking her head. 'Really darling.' I tried to show by my expression that I perhaps couldn't read the inscription without eyeglasses; I squinted, neutrally. Mrs Silsburn seemed reluctant to hand the folder back to its owner. When she had, and the Lieutenant had replaced the folder in the breast pocket of his tunic, she said, 'I don't think I've ever seen that before.' Turned almost completely around, now, in her jump seat, she sat gazing rather fondly at the Lieutenant's breast pocket.

'We had a whole bunch of them made up last year,' the Lieutenant said. 'Be amazed, actually, how it keeps you from running out of matches.'

The Matron of Honor turned to him – or, rather, on him. 'We didn't do it for *that*,' she said. She gave Mrs Silsburn a you-know-how-men-are look, and said to her, 'I don't know. I just thought it was cute. Corny, but sort of cute. You know.'

'It's darling. I don't think I've ever –'

'Actually, it isn't original or anything like that. Everybody's got them now,' the Matron of Honor said. 'Where I got the idea originally, as a matter of fact, was from Muriel's mother and dad. They always had them around the house.' She inhaled deeply on her cigarette, and as she went on talking, she released the smoke in little syllabic drafts. '*Golly*, they're terrific people. That's what *kills* me about this whole business. I mean why doesn't something like this happen to all the stinkers in the world, instead of the nice ones? That's what I can't understand.' She looked to Mrs Silsburn for an answer.

Mrs Silsburn smiled a smile that was at once worldly, wan, and enigmatic – the smile, as I remember, of a sort of jump-seat Mona Lisa. 'I've often wondered,' she mused softly. She then mentioned, rather ambiguously, 'Muriel's mother is my late husband's baby sister, you know.'

'Oh!' the Matron of Honor said with interest. 'Well, then, *you know*.' She reached out an extraordinarily long left arm, and flicked her cigarette ashes into the ashtray near her husband's window. 'I honestly think she's one of the few really brilliant people I've met in my entire life. I mean she's read just about everything that's ever been printed. My gosh, if I'd read just about one-tenth of what that woman's read and forg*ot*ten, I'd be happy. I mean she's *taught*, she's worked on a *news*paper, she designs her own *clothes*, she does every single bit of her own *house*work. Her cooking's out of this *world*. Golly! I honestly think she's the most wonder –'

'Did she approve of the marriage?' Mrs Silsburn interrupted. 'I mean the reason I ask, I've been in Detroit for weeks and weeks. My sister-in-law suddenly passed away, and I've –'

'She's too nice to say,' the Matron of Honor said flatly. She shook her head. 'I mean she's too – you know – dis*creet* and all.' She reflected. 'As a matter of fact, this morning's about the only time I ever heard her say boo on the subject, really. And then it was only just because she was so upset about poor Muriel.' She reached out an arm and tipped her cigarette ashes again.

'What'd she say this morning?' Mrs Silsburn asked avidly.

The Matron of Honor seemed to reflect for a moment. 'Well, nothing very much, really,' she said. 'I mean nothing small or really de*ro*gatory or anything like that. All she said, really, was that this Seymour, in her opinion, was a latent homosexual and that he was basically afraid of marriage. I mean she didn't say it nasty or anything. She just said it – you know – intelligently. I mean she was psychoanalyzed herself for years and years.' The Matron of Honor looked at Mrs Silsburn. 'That's no *secret* or anything. I mean Mrs Fedder'll tell you that herself, so I'm not giving away any secret or anything.'

'I know that,' Mrs Silsburn said quickly. 'She's the last person in the –'

'I mean the point is,' the Matron of Honor said, 'she isn't the kind of person that comes right out and says something like that unless she knows what she's talking about. And she never, never would've said it in the *first* place if poor Muriel hadn't been so – you know – so prostrate and everything.' She shook her head grimly. 'Golly, you should've seen that poor kid.'

I should, no doubt, break in here to describe my general reaction to the main import of what the Matron of Honor was saying. I'd just as soon let it go, though, for the moment, if the reader will bear with me.

'What else did she say?' Mrs Silsburn asked. 'Rhea, I mean. Did she say anything else?' I didn't look at her – I couldn't take my eyes off the Matron of Honor's face – but I had a passing, wild impression that Mrs Silsburn was all but sitting in the main speaker's lap.

'No. Not really. Hardly anything.' The Matron of Honor, reflecting, shook her head. 'I mean, as I say, she wouldn't have said *any*thing – with people standing around and all – if poor Muriel hadn't been so crazy upset.' She flicked her cigarette ashes again. 'About the only other thing she said was that this Seymour was a really schizoid personality and that, if you really looked at it the right way, it was really better for Muriel that things turned out the way they did. Which makes sense to *me*, but I'm not so sure it does to Muriel. He's got her so *buffaloed* that she doesn't know whether she's coming or going. That's what makes me so –'

She was interrupted at that point. By me. As I remember, my voice was unsteady, as it invariably is when I'm vastly upset.

'What brought Mrs Fedder to the conclusion that Seymour is a latent homosexual and a schizoid personality?'

All eyes – all searchlights, it seemed – the Matron of Honor's,

Mrs Silsburn's, even the Lieutenant's, were abruptly trained on me. 'What?' the Matron of Honor said to me, sharply, faintly hostilely. And again I had a passing, abrasive notion that she knew I was Seymour's brother.

'What makes Mrs Fedder think that Seymour's a latent homosexual and schizoid personality?'

The Matron of Honor stared at me, then gave an eloquent snort. She turned and appealed to Mrs Silsburn with a maximum of irony. 'Would you say that somebody's *norm*al that pulled a stunt like the one today?' She raised her eyebrows, and waited. 'Would you?' she asked quietly-quietly. 'Be honest. I'm just asking. For this gentleman's benefit.'

Mrs Silsburn's answer was gentleness itself, fairness itself. 'No, I certainly would not,' she said.

I had a sudden, violent impulse to jump out of the car and break into a sprint, in any direction at all. As I remember, though, I was still in my jump seat when the Matron of Honor addressed me again. 'Look,' she said, in the spuriously patient tone of voice that a teacher might take with a child who is not only retarded but whose nose is forever running unattractively. 'I don't know how much you know about people. But what man in his right mind, the night before he's supposed to get married, keeps his fiancée up all night blabbing to her all about how he's too *happy* to get married and that she'll have to post*pone* the wedding till he feels *steadier* or he won't be able to come to it? *Then*, when his fiancée explains to him like a *child* that everything's been arranged and planned out for months, and that her father's gone to incredible expense and trouble and all to have a reception and everything like that, and that her relatives and friends are coming from all over the *country* – *then*, after she explains all that, he says to her he's terribly sorry but he can't get married till he feels less *happy* or some crazy thing! Use your head, now, if you don't mind. Does that sound like somebody *normal*? Does that sound like somebody in their right mind?' Her voice was now shrill. 'Or does that sound like somebody that should be stuck in some booby hatch?' She looked at me very severely, and when I didn't immediately speak up in either defense or surrender, she sat heavily back in her seat, and said to her husband, 'Give me another cigarette, please. This thing's gonna burn me.' She handed him her burning stub, and he extinguished it for her. He then took out his cigarette package again. 'You light it,' she said. 'I haven't got the energy.'

Mrs Silsburn cleared her throat. 'It sounds to me,' she said, 'like a blessing in disguise that everything's turned –'

'I ask *you*,' the Matron of Honor said to her with a fresh impetus, at the same time accepting a freshly lighted cigarette from her husband. 'Does that sound like a normal person – a normal *man* – to you? Or does it sound like somebody that's either never *grown up* or is just an absolute raving maniac of some crazy kind?'

'Goodness. I don't know what to say, really. It just sounds to me like a blessing in disguise that every –'

The Matron of Honor sat forward suddenly, alertly, exhaling smoke through her nostrils. 'All right, never mind that, drop that for a minute – I don't need that,' she said. She was addressing Mrs Silsburn, but in actuality she was addressing me through Mrs Silsburn's face, so to speak. 'Did you ever see — —, in the movies?' she demanded.

The name she mentioned was the professional name of a then fairly well-known – and now, in 1955, a quite famous – actress-singer.

'Yes,' said Mrs Silsburn quickly and interestedly, and waited.

The Matron of Honor nodded. 'All right,' she said. 'Did you ever notice, by any chance, how she smiles sort of crooked? Only on one side of her face, sort of? It's very noticeable if you –'

'*Yes* – yes, I have!' Mrs Silsburn said.

The Matron of Honor dragged on her cigarette, and glanced over – just perceptibly – at me. 'Well, that happens to be a partial par*al*ysis of some kind,' she said, exhaling a little gust of smoke with each word. 'And do you know how she got it? This *normal* Seymour person apparently hit her and she had nine stitches taken in her face.' She reached over (in lieu, possibly, of a better stage direction) and flicked her ashes again.

'May I ask where you heard that?' I said. My lips were quivering slightly, like two fools.

'You may,' she said, looking at Mrs Silsburn instead of me. 'Muriel's mother happened to mention it about two hours ago, while Muriel was sobbing her eyes out. She looked at me. 'Does that answer your question?' She suddenly shifted her bouquet of gardenias from her right to her left hand. It was the nearest thing to a fairly commonplace nervous gesture that I'd seen her make. 'Just for your information, incidentally,' she said, looking at me, 'do you know who I think you are? I think you're this Seymour's brother.' She waited, very briefly, and, when I didn't say anything: 'You *look* like him, from his crazy picture, and I happen to know that he was supposed to come to the wedding. His sister or somebody told Muriel.' Her look was fixed unwaveringly on my face. 'Are you?' she asked bluntly.

My voice must have sounded a trifle rented when I answered. 'Yes,' I said. My face was burning. In a way, though, I felt an infinitely less furry sense of self-identification than I had since I'd got off the train earlier in the afternoon.

'I *knew* you were,' the Matron of Honor said. 'I'm not *stup*id, you know. I knew who you were the minute you got in this car.' She turned to her husband. 'Didn't I say he was his brother the minute he got in this car? Didn't I?'

The Lieutenant altered his sitting position a trifle. 'Well, you said he probably – yes, you did,' he said. 'You did. Yes.'

One didn't have to look over at Mrs Silsburn to perceive how attentively she had taken in this latest development. I glanced past and behind her, furtively, at the fifth passenger – the tiny elderly man – to see if his insularity was still intact. It was. No one's indifference has ever been such a comfort to me.

The Matron of Honor came back to me. 'For your information, I also know that your brother's no chiro*p*odist. So don't be so funny. I happen to know he was Billy Black on 'It's a Wise Child' for about fifty *years* or something.'

Mrs Silsburn abruptly took a more active part in the conversation. 'The radio program?' she inquired, and I felt her looking at me with a fresh, keener, interest.

The Matron of Honor didn't answer her. 'Which one were *you*?' she said to me. '*Georgie* Black?' The mixture of rudeness and curiosity in her voice was interesting, if not quite disarming.

'Georgie Black was my brother Walt,' I said, answering only her second question.

She turned to Mrs Silsburn. 'It's supposed to be some kind of a *secret* or something, but this man and his brother *Sey*mour were on this radio program under fake names or something. The *Black* children.'

'Take it easy, honey, take it easy,' the Lieutenant suggested, rather nervously.

His wife turned to him. 'I will *not* take it easy,' she said – and again, contrary to my every conscious inclination, I felt a little pinch of something close to admiration for her metal, solid brass or no. 'His brother's supposed to be so in*tell*igent, for heaven's sake,' she said. 'In college when he was *fourteen* or something, and all like that. If what he did to that kid today is intelligent, then I'm Mahatma Gandhi! I don't care. It just makes me sick!'

Just then, I felt a minute extra added discomfort. Someone was very closely examining the left, or weaker, side of my face. It was Mrs Silsburn. She started a bit as I turned abruptly toward her. 'May I ask if you were Buddy Black?' she said, and a certain deferential note in her voice rather made me think, for a fractional moment, that she was about to present me with a fountain pen and a small, morocco-bound autograph album. The passing thought made me distinctly uneasy – considering, if nothing else, the fact that it was 1942 and some nine or ten years past my commercial bloom. 'The reason I ask,' she said, 'my husband used to listen to that program without fail every single –'

'If you're interested,' the Matron of Honor interrupted her, looking at me, 'that was the one program on the air I always absolutely loathed. I loathe precocious children. If I ever had a child that –'

The end of her sentence was lost to us. She was interrupted, suddenly and unequivocally, by the most piercing, most deafening, most *impure* E-flat blast I've ever heard. All of us in the car, I'm sure, literally jumped. At that moment, a drum-and-bugle corps, composed of what seemed to be a hundred or more tone-deaf Sea

Scouts, was passing. With what seemed to be almost delinquent abandon, the boys had just rammed into the sides of 'The Stars and Stripes Forever.' Mrs Silsburn, very sensibly, clapped her hands over her ears.

For an eternity of seconds, it seemed, the din was all but incredible. Only the Matron of Honor's voice could have risen above it – or, for that matter, would have attempted to. When it did, one might have thought she was addressing us, obviously at the top of her voice, from some great distance away, somewhere, possibly, in the vicinity of the bleachers of Yankee Stadium.

'I can't take this!' she said. 'Let's get out of here and find some place to *phone* from! I've got to phone Muriel and say we're delayed! She'll be crazy!'

With the advent of the local Armageddon, Mrs Silsburn and I had faced front to see it in. We now turned around again in our jump seats to face the Leader. And, possibly, our deliverer.

'There's a Schrafft's on Seventy-ninth Street!' she bellowed at Mrs Silsburn. 'Let's go have a *soda*, and I can *phone* from there! It'll at least be air-conditioned!'

Mrs Silsburn nodded enthusiastically, and pantomimed 'Yes!' with her mouth.

'You come, too!' the Matron of Honor shouted at me.

With *very* peculiar spontaneity, I remember, I shouted back to her the altogether extravagant word 'Fine!' (It isn't easy, to this day, to account for the Matron of Honor's having included me in her invitation to quit the ship. It may simply have been inspired by a born leader's natural sense of orderliness. She may have had some sort of remote but compulsive urge to make her landing party complete . . . My singularly immediate acceptance of the invitation strikes me as much more easily explainable. I prefer to think it was a basically religious impulse. In certain Zen monasteries, it's a cardinal rule, if not the only serious enforced discipline, that when one monk calls out 'Hi!' to another monk, the latter must call back 'Hi!' without thinking.)

The Matron of Honor then turned and, for the first time, directly addressed the tiny elderly man beside her. To my undying gratification, he was still glaring straight ahead of him, as though his own private scenery hadn't changed an iota. His unlighted clear-Havana cigar was still clenched between two fingers. What with his apparent unmindfulness of the terrible din the passing drum-and-bugle corps was making, and, possibly, from a grim tenet that all old men over eighty must be either stone-deaf or very hard of hearing, the Matron of Honor brought her lips to within an inch or two of his left ear. 'We're going to get out of the car!' she shouted at him – almost into him. 'We're going to find a place to *phone* from, and maybe have some refreshment! Do you want to come with us?'

The elderly man's immediate reaction was just short of glorious. He looked first at the Matron of Honor, then at the rest of us, and then grinned. It was a grin that was no less resplendent for the fact that it made no sense whatever. Nor for the fact that his teeth were obviously, beautifully, transcendently false. He looked at the Matron of Honor inquisitively for just an instant, his grin wonderfully intact. Or, rather, he looked *to* her – as if, I thought, he believed the Matron of Honor, or one of us, had lovely plans to pass a picnic basket his way.

'I don't think he heard you, honey!' the Lieutenant shouted.

The Matron of Honor nodded, and once again brought the megaphone of her mouth up close to the old man's ear. With really praiseworthy volume, she repeated her invitation to the old man to join us in quitting the car. Once again, at face value, the old man seemed more than amenable to any suggestion in the world – possibly not short of trotting over and having a dip in the East River. But again, too, one had an uneasy conviction that he hadn't heard a word that was said to him. Abruptly, he proved that this was true. With an enormous grin at all of us collectively, he raised his cigar hand and, with one finger, significantly tapped first his mouth, then his ear. The gesture, as *he* made it, seemed related to a perfectly first-class joke of some kind that he fully meant to share with all of us.

At that moment, Mrs Silsburn, beside me, gave a visible little sign – almost a jump – of comprehension. She touched the Matron of Honor's pink satin arm, and shouted, 'I know who he is! He's deaf and dumb – he's a deaf-mute! He's Muriel's father's uncle!'

The Matron of Honor's lips formed the word 'Oh!' She swung around in her seat, toward her husband. 'You got a pencil and paper?' she bellowed to him.

I touched her arm and shouted that *I* had. Hastily – almost, in fact, for some reason, as though time were about to run out on all of us – I took out of my inside tunic pocket a small pad and a pencil stub that I'd recently acquisitioned from a desk drawer of my company Orderly Room at Fort Benning.

Somewhat overly legibly, I wrote on a sheet of paper, 'We're held up indefinitely by the parade. We're going to find a phone and have a cold drink somewhere. Will you join us?' I folded the paper once, then handed it to the Matron of Honor, who opened it, read it, and then handed it to the tiny old man. He read it, grinning, and then looked at me and wagged his head up and down several times vehemently. I thought for an instant that this was the full and perfectly eloquent extent of his reply, but he suddenly motioned to me with his hand, and I gathered that he wanted me to pass him my pad and pencil. I did so – without looking over at the Matron of Honor, from whom great waves of impatience were rising. The old man adjusted the pad and pencil on his lap with the greatest care, then sat for a moment, pencil poised, in obvious concentration, his grin diminished only a very trifle. Then the pencil began, very unsteadily, to move. An 'i' was dotted. And then both pad and pencil were returned personally to me, with a marvellously cordial extra added wag of the head. He had written, in letters that had not quite jelled yet, the single word 'Delighted.' The Matron of Honor, reading over my shoulder, gave a sound faintly like a snort, but I quickly looked over at the great writer and tried to show by my expression that all of us in the car knew a poem when we saw one, and were grateful.

One by one, then, from both doors, we all got out of the car – abandoned ship, as it were, in the middle of Madison Avenue, in a sea of hot, gummy macadam. The Lieutenant lingered behind a moment to inform the driver of our mutiny. As I remember very well, the drum-and-bugle corps was still endlessly passing, and the din hadn't abated a bit.

The Matron of Honor and Mrs Silsburn led the way to Schrafft's. They walked as a twosome – almost as advance scouts – south on the east side of Madison Avenue. When he'd finished briefing the driver, the Lieutenant caught up with them. Or almost up with them. He fell a little behind them, in order to take out his wallet in privacy and see, apparently, how much money he had with him.

The bride's father's uncle and I brought up the rear. Whether he had intuited that I was his friend or simply because I was the owner of a pad and pencil, he had rather more scrambled than gravitated to a walking position beside me. The very top of his beautiful silk hat didn't quite come up as high as my shoulder. I set a comparatively slow gait for us, in deference to the length of his legs. At the end of a block or so, we were quite a good distance behind the others. I don't think it troubled either of us. Occasionally, I remember, as we walked along, my friend and I looked up and down, respectively, at each other and exchanged idiotic expressions of pleasure at sharing one another's company.

When my companion and I reached the revolving door of Schrafft's Seventy-ninth Street, the Matron of Honor, her husband, and Mrs Silsburn had all been standing there for some minutes. They were waiting, I thought, as a rather forbiddingly integrated party of three. They had been talking, but they stopped when our motley twosome approached. In the car, just a couple of minutes earlier, when the drum-and-bugle corps blasted by, a common discomfort, almost a common anguish, had lent our small group a semblance of alliance – of the sort that can be temporarily conferred on Cook's tourists caught in a very heavy rainstorm at Pompeii. All too clearly now, as the tiny old man and I reached the revolving door of Schrafft's, the storm was over. The Matron of Honor and I exchanged expressions of recognition, not of greeting. 'It's closed for alterations,' she stated coldly, looking at me. Unofficially but unmistakably, she was appointing me odd-man-out again, and at that moment, for no reason worth going into, I felt a sense of isolation and loneliness more overwhelming than I'd felt all day. Somewhat simultaneously, it's worth noting, my cough reactivated itself. I pulled my handkerchief out of my hip pocket. The Matron of Honor turned to Mrs Silsburn and her husband. 'There's a Longchamps around here *some*where,' she said, 'but I don't know where.'

'I don't either,' Mrs Silsburn said. She seemed very close to tears. At both her forehead and her upper lip, perspiration had seeped through even her heavy pancake makeup. A black patent leather handbag was under her left arm. She held it as though it were a favorite doll, and she herself an experimentally rouged and powdered, and very unhappy, runaway child.

'We're not gonna be able to get a cab for love or money,' the Lieutenant said pessimistically. He was looking the worse for wear, too. His 'hot pilot's' cap appeared almost cruelly incongruous on his pale, dripping, deeply unintrepid-looking face, and I remember having an impulse to whisk it off his head, or at least to straighten it somewhat, to adjust it into a less cocked position – the same impulse, in general motive, that one might feel at a children's party, where there is invariably one small, exceedingly homely child wearing a paper hat that crushes down one or both ears.

'Oh, God, what a day!' the Matron of Honor said for all of us. Her circlet of artificial flowers was somewhat askew, and she was thoroughly damp, but, I thought, the only thing really destructible about her was her remotest appendage, so to speak – her gardenia bouquet. She was still holding it, however absent-mindedly, in her hand. It obviously hadn't stood the gaff. 'What'll we *do*?' she asked, rather frantically, for her. 'We can't *walk* there. They live practically in *River*dale. Does anybody have any bright ideas?' She looked first at Mrs Silsburn, then at her husband – and then, in desperation possibly, at me.

'I have an apartment near here,' I said suddenly and nervously. 'It's just down the block, as a matter of fact.' I have a feeling that I gave out this information a trifle too loudly. I may even have shouted it, for all I know. 'It belongs to my brother and me. My sister's using it while we're in the army, but she's not there now. She's in the Waves, and she's off on some trip.' I looked at the

Matron of Honor – or at some point just over her head. 'You can at least phone from there, if you like,' I said. 'And the apartment's air-conditioned. We might all cool off for a minute and get our breaths.'

When the first shock of the invitation had passed over, the Matron of Honor, Mrs Silsburn, and the Lieutenant went into a sort of consultation, of eyes only, but there was no visible sign that any kind of verdict was forthcoming. The Matron of Honor was the first to take any kind of action. She'd been looking – in vain – at the other two for an opinion on the subject. She turned back to me and said, 'Did you say you had a phone?'

'Yes. Unless my sister's had it disconnected for some reason, and I can't see why she would have.'

'How do we know your *brother* won't be there?' the Matron of Honor said.

It was a small consideration that hadn't entered my overheated head. 'I don't think he will be,' I said. 'He *may* be – it's his apartment, too – but I don't think he will. I really don't.'

The Matron of Honor stared at me, openly, for a moment – and not really rudely, for a change, unless children's stares are rude. Then she turned back to her husband and Mrs Silsburn, and said, 'We might as well. At least we can phone.' They nodded in agreement. Mrs Silsburn, in fact, went so far as to remember her code of etiquette covering invitations given in front of Schrafft's. Through her sun-baked pancake makeup, a semblance of an Emily Post smile peeped out at me. It was very welcome, as I remember. 'C'mon, then, let's get out of this *sun*,' our leader said. 'What'll I do with *this*?' She didn't wait for an answer. She stepped over to the curb and unsentimentally disengaged herself from her wilted gardenia bouquet. 'O.K., lead on, Macduff,' she said to me. 'We'll follow you. And all I have to say is he'd better *not* be there when we get there, or I'll kill the bastard.' She looked at Mrs Silsburn. 'Excuse my language – but I mean it.'

As directed, I took the lead, almost happily. An instant later, a silk hat materialized in the air beside me, considerably down and at the left, and my special, only technically unassigned cohort grinned up at me – for a moment, I rather thought he was going to slip his hand into mine.

My three guests and my one friend remained outside in the hall while I briefly cased the apartment.

The windows were all closed, the two air-conditioners had been turned to 'Shut,' and the first breath one took was rather like inhaling deeply in someone's ancient racoon-coat pocket. The only sound in the whole apartment was the somewhat trembling purr of the aged refrigerator Seymour and I had acquired second-hand. My sister Boo Boo, in her girlish, naval way, had left it turned on. There were, in fact, throughout the apartment, any number of little untidy signs that a seafaring lady had taken over the place. A handsome, small-size, ensign's navy-blue jacket was flung, lining down, across the couch. A box of Louis Sherry candies – half empty, and with the unconsumed candies all more or less experimentally squeezed – was open on the coffee table, in front of the couch. A framed photograph of a very resolute-looking young man I'd never seen before stood on the desk. And all the ashtrays in sight were in full blossom with crumpled facial tissues and lipsticked cigarette ends. I didn't go into the kitchen, the bedroom, or the bathroom, except to open the doors and take a quick look to see if Seymour was standing upright anywhere. For one reason, I felt enervated and lazy. For another, I was kept pretty busy raising blinds, turning on air-conditioners, emptying loaded ashtrays. Besides, the other members of the party barged in on me almost immediately. 'It's hotter in here than it is on the street,' the Matron of Honor said, by way of greeting, as she strode in.

'I'll be with you in just a minute,' I said. 'I can't seem to get this air-conditioner to work.' The 'On' button seemed to be stuck, in fact, and I was busily tinkering with it.

While I worked on the air-conditioner switch – with my hat still on my head, I remember – the others circulated rather suspiciously around the room. I watched them out of the corner of one eye. The Lieutenant went over to the desk and stood looking up at the three or four square feet of wall directly above it, where my brother and I, for defiantly sentimental reasons, had tacked up a number of glossy eight-by-ten photographs. Mrs Silsburn sat down – inevitably, I thought – in the one chair in the room that my deceased Boston bull used to enjoy sleeping in; its arms, upholstered in dirty corduroy, had been thoroughly slavered and chewed on in the course of many a nightmare. The bride's father's uncle – my great friend – seemed to have disappeared completely. The Matron of Honor, too, seemed suddenly to be somewhere else. 'I'll get you all something to drink in just a second,' I said uneasily, still trying to force the switch button on the air-conditioner.

'I could use something cold to drink,' said a very familiar voice. I turned completely around and saw that she had stretched herself out on the couch, which accounted for her noticeable vertical disappearance. 'I'll use your phone in just a second,' she advised me. 'I couldn't open my mouth anyway to talk on the phone, in this condition, I'm so parched. My *tongue's* so dry.'

The air-conditioner abruptly whirred into operation, and I came over to the middle of the room, into the space between the couch and the chair where Mrs Silsburn was sitting. 'I don't know what there is to drink,' I said. 'I haven't looked in the refrigerator, but I imagine –'

'Bring *any*thing,' the eternal spokeswoman interrupted from the couch. 'Just make it wet. And *cold*.' The heels of her shoes were resting on the sleeve of my sister's jacket. Her hands were folded across her chest. A pillow was bunched up under her head. 'Put ice in it, if you have any,' she said, and closed her eyes. I looked down at her for a brief but murderous instant, then bent over and, as tactfully as possible, eased Boo Boo's jacket out from under her feet. I started to leave the room and go about my chores as host, but just as I took a step, the Lieutenant spoke up from over at the desk.

'Whereja get all these pictures?' he said.

I went directly over to him. I was still wearing my visored, oversize garrison cap. It hadn't occurred to me to take it off. I stood beside him at the desk, and yet a trifle behind him, and looked up at the photographs on the wall. I said they were mostly old pictures of the children who had been on 'It's a Wise Child' in the days when Seymour and I had been on the show.

The Lieutenant turned to me. 'What was it?' he said. 'I never heard it. One of those kids' quiz shows? Questions and answers, and like that?' Unmistakably, a soupçon of Army rank had slipped unnoisily but insidiously into his voice. He also seemed to be looking at my hat.

I took off my hat, and said, 'No, not exactly.' A certain amount of low family pride was suddenly evoked. 'It *was* before my brother Seymour was on it. And it more or less got that way again after he went off the program. But he changed the whole format, really. He turned the program into a kind of children's round-table discussion.'

The Lieutenant looked at me with, I thought, somewhat excessive interest. 'Were you on it, too?' he said.

'Yes.'

The Matron of Honor spoke up from the other side of the room, from the invisible, dusty recesses of the couch. 'I'd like to see a kid of *mine* get on one of those crazy programs,' she said. 'Or *act*. Any of those things. I'd die, in fact, before I'd let any child of mine turn themself into a little exhibitionist before the public. It warps their whole entire lives. The pub*lic*ity and all, if nothing else – ask any psychiatrist. I mean how can you have any kind of a normal *child*hood or anything?' Her head, crowned in a now lopsided circlet of flowers, suddenly popped into view. As though disembodied, it perched on the catwalk of the back of the couch, facing the Lieutenant and me. 'That's probably what's the matter with that brother of yours,' the Head said. 'I mean you lead an absolutely freakish life like that when you're a kid, and so naturally you never learn to grow up. You never learn to relate to normal people or anything. That's exactly what Mrs Fedder was saying in that crazy bedroom a couple of hours ago. But exactly. Your brother's never learned to relate to anybody. All he can do, apparently, is go around giving people a bunch of stitches in their faces. He's absolutely unfit for marriage or *any*thing halfway normal, for goodness' sake. As a matter of fact, that's *exactly* what Mrs Fedder said.' The Head then turned just enough to glare over at the Lieutenant. 'Am I right, Bob? Did she or didn't she say that? Tell the truth.'

The next voice to speak up was not the Lieutenant's but mine. My mouth was dry, and my groin felt damp. I said I didn't give a good God damn what Mrs Fedder had to say on the subject of Seymour. Or, for that matter, what any professional dilettante or amateur bitch had to say. I said that from the time Seymour was ten years old, every *summa-cum-laude* Thinker and intellectual men's-room attendant in the country had been having a go at him. I said it might be different if Seymour had just been some nasty little high-I.Q. showoff. I said he hadn't ever been an exhibitionist. He went down to the broadcast every Wednesday night as though he were going to his own funeral. He didn't even talk to you, for God's sake, the whole way down on the bus or subway. I said that not one God-damn person, of all the patronizing, fourth-rate critics and column writers, had ever seen him for what he really was. A poet, for God's sake. And I mean a *poet*. If he never wrote a line of poetry, he could still flash what he had at you with the back of his ear if he wanted to.

I stopped right there, thank God. My heart was banging away something terrible, and, like most hypochondriacs, I had a little passing, intimidating notion that such speeches were the stuff that heart attacks are made of. To this day, I have no idea at all how my guests reacted to my outbreak, the polluted little stream of invective I'd loosed on them. The first real exterior detail that I was aware of was the universally familiar sound of plumbing. It came from another part of the apartment. I looked around the room suddenly, between and through and past the immediate faces of my guests. 'Where's the old man?' I asked. 'The little old man?' Butter wouldn't have melted in my mouth.

Oddly enough, when an answer came, it came from the Lieutenant, not the Matron of Honor. 'I believe he's in the bathroom,' he said. The statement was issued with a special forthrightness, proclaiming the speaker to be one of those who don't mince everyday hygienic facts.

'Oh,' I said. I looked rather absently around the room again. Whether or not I deliberately avoided meeting the Matron of

Honor's terrible eye, I don't remember, or don't care to remember. I spotted the bride's father's uncle's silk hat on the seat of a straight chair, across the room. I had an impulse to say hello, aloud, to it. 'I'll get some cold drinks,' I said. 'I'll just be a minute.'

'May I use your phone?' the Matron of Honor suddenly said to me as I passed by the couch. She swung her feet to the floor.

'Yes – yes, of course,' I said. I looked at Mrs Silsburn and the Lieutenant. 'I thought I'd make some Tom Collinses, if there are any lemons or limes. Will that be all right?'

The Lieutenant's answer startled me by its sudden conviviality. 'Bring 'em on,' he said, and rubbed his hands together, like a hearty drinking man.

Mrs Silsburn left off studying the photographs over the desk to advise me, 'If you're going to make Tom Collinses – please, just a teentsy, teentsy little bit of gin in mine. Almost none at all, if it isn't too much trouble.' She was beginning to look a bit recuperated, even in just the short time since we'd got off the street. Perhaps, for one reason, because she was standing within a few feet of the air-conditioner I'd turned on and some cool air was coming her way. I said I'd look out for her drink, and then left her among the minor radio 'celebrities' of the early thirties and the late twenties, the many passé little faces of Seymour's and my boyhood. The Lieutenant seemed well able to shift for himself in my absence, too; he was already moving, hands joined behind his back, like a lone connoisseur, toward the bookshelves. The Matron of Honor followed me out of the room, yawning as she did – a cavernous, audible yawn that she made no effort to suppress or obstruct from view.

As the Matron of Honor followed me toward the bedroom, where the phone was, the bride's father's uncle came toward us from the far end of the hall. His face was in the ferocious repose that had fooled me during most of the car ride, but as he came closer to us in the hall, the mask reversed itself; he pantomimed to us both the very highest salutations and greetings, and I found myself grinning and nodding immoderately in return. His sparse white hair looked freshly combed – almost freshly washed, as though he might have discovered a tiny barbershop cached away at the other end of the apartment. When he'd passed us, I felt a compulsion to look back over my shoulder, and when I did, he waved to me, vigorously – a great, *bon-voyage*, come-back-soon wave. It picked me up no end. 'What is he? Crazy?' the Matron of Honor said. I said I hoped so, and opened the door of the bedroom.

She sat down heavily on one of the twin beds – Seymour's, as a matter of fact. The phone was on the night table within easy reach. I said I'd bring her a drink right away. 'Don't bother – I'll be right out,' she said. 'Just close the door, if you don't mind . . . I don't mean it that way, but I can never talk on the phone unless the door's closed.' I told her I was the exact same way, and started to leave. But just as I'd turned to come out of the space between the two beds, I noticed a small collapsible canvas valise over on the window seat. At first glance, I thought it was mine, miraculously arrived at the apartment, all the way from Penn Station, under its own steam. My second thought was that it must be Boo Boo's. I walked over to it. It was unzipped, and just one look at the top layer of its contents told me who the real owner was. With another, more inclusive look, I saw something lying on top of two laundered suntan shirts that I thought ought not to be left alone in the room with the Matron of Honor. I picked it out of the bag, slipped it under one arm, waved fraternally to the Matron of Honor, who had already inserted a finger into the first hole of the number she intended to dial, and was waiting for me to clear out, and then I closed the door behind me.

I stood for some little time outside the bedroom, in the gracious solitude of the hall, wondering what to do with Seymour's diary, which, I ought to rush to say, was the object I'd picked out of the top of the canvas bag. My first constructive thought was to hide it till my guests had left. It seemed to me a good idea to take it into the bathroom and drop it into the laundry hamper. However, on a second and much more involved train of thought, I decided to take it into the bathroom and read parts of it and *then* drop it into the laundry hamper.

It was a day, God knows, not only of rampant signs and

symbols but of wildly extensive communication via the written word. If you jumped into crowded cars, Fate took circuitous pains, before you did any jumping, that you had a pad and pencil with you, just in case one of your fellow-passengers was a deaf-mute. If you slipped into bathrooms, you did well to look up to see if there were any little messages, faintly apocalyptical or otherwise, posted high over the washbowl.

For years, among the seven children in our one-bathroom family, it was our perhaps cloying but serviceable custom to leave messages for one another on the medicine-cabinet mirror, using a moist sliver of soap to write with. The general theme of our messages usually ran to excessively strong admonitions and, not infrequently, undisguised threats. 'Boo Boo, pick up your washcloth when you're done with it. Don't leave it on the floor. Love, Seymour.' 'Walt, your turn to take Z. and F. to the park. I did it yesterday. Guess who.' 'Wednesday is their anniversary. Don't go to movies or hang around studio after broadcast or pay forfeit. This means you, too, Buddy.' 'Mother said Zooey nearly ate the Feenolax. Don't leave slightly poisonous objects on the sink that he can reach and eat.' These, of course, are samples straight out of our childhood, but years later, when, in the name of independence or what-have-you, Seymour and I branched out and took an apartment of our own, he and I had not more than nominally departed from the old family custom. That is, we didn't just throw away our old soap fragments.

When I'd checked into the bathroom with Seymour's diary under my arm, and had carefully secured the door behind me, I spotted a message almost immediately. It was not, however, in Seymour's handwriting but, unmistakably, in my sister Boo Boo's. With or without soap, her handwriting was always almost indecipherably minute, and she had easily managed to post the following message up on the mirror: 'Raise high the roof beam, carpenters. Like Ares comes the bridegroom, taller far than a tall man. Love, Irving Sappho, formerly under contract to Elysium Studios Ltd. Please be happy happy *happy* with your beautiful Muriel. This is an order. I outrank everybody on this block.' The contract writer quoted in the text, I might mention, has always been a great favorite – at appropriately staggered time intervals – with all the children in our family, largely through the immeasurable impact of Seymour's taste in poetry on all of us. I read and reread the quotation, and then I sat down on the edge of the bathtub and opened Seymour's diary.

What follows is an exact reproduction of the pages from Seymour's diary that I read while I was sitting on the edge of the bathtub. It seems perfectly orderly to me to leave out individual datelines. Suffice it to say, I think, all these entries were made while he was stationed at Fort Monmouth, in late 1941 and early 1942, some several months before the wedding date was set.

'It was freezing cold at retreat parade this evening, and yet about six men from our platoon alone fainted during the endless playing of "The Star-Spangled Banner." I suppose if your blood circulation is normal, you can't take the unnatural military position of attention. Especially if you're holding a leaden rifle up at Present Arms. I have no circulation, no pulse. Immobility is my home. The tempo of "The Star-Spangled Banner" and I are in perfect understanding. To me, its rhythm is a romantic waltz.

'We got passes till midnight, after the parade. I met Muriel at the Biltmore at seven. Two drinks, two drugstore tuna-fish sandwiches, then a movie she wanted to see, something with Greer Garson in it. I looked at her several times in the dark when Greer Garson's son's plane was missing in action. Her mouth was open. Absorbed, worried. The identification with Metro-Goldwyn-Mayer tragedy complete. I felt awe and happiness. How I love and need her undiscriminating heart. She looked over at me when the children in the picture brought in the kitten to show to their mother. M. loved the kitten and wanted me to love it. Even in the dark, I could sense that she felt the usual estrangement from me when I don't automatically love what she loves. Later, when we were having a drink at the station, she asked me if I didn't think that kitten was "rather nice." She doesn't use the word "cute" any more. When did I ever frighten her out of her normal vocabulary? Bore that I am, I mentioned R. H. Blyth's definition of sentimentality: that we are being sentimental when we give to a thing more tenderness than God gives to it. I said (sententiously?) that God undoubtedly loves kittens, but not, in all probability, with Technicolor bootees on their paws. He leaves that creative touch to script writers. M. thought this over, seemed to agree with me, but the "knowledge" wasn't too very welcome. She sat stirring her drink and feeling unclose to me. She worries over the way her love for me comes and goes, appears and disappears. She doubts its reality simply because it isn't as steadily pleasurable as a kitten. God knows it *is* sad. The human voice conspires to desecrate everything on earth.'

'Dinner tonight at the Fedders'. Very good. Veal, mashed potatoes, lima beans, a beautiful oil-and-vinegar green salad. For dessert there was something Muriel made herself: a kind of frozen cream-cheese affair, with raspberries on it. It made tears come to my eyes. (Saigyo says, "What it is I know not/But with the gratitude/My tears fall.") A bottle of ketchup was placed on the table near me. Muriel apparently told Mrs Fedder that I put ketchup on everything. I'd give the world to have seen M. telling her mother defensively that I put ketchup even on string beans. My precious girl.

'After dinner Mrs Fedder suggested we listen to the program. Her enthusiasm, her nostalgia for the program, especially for the old days when Buddy and I were on it, makes me uneasy. Tonight it was broadcast from some naval airbase, of all places, near San Diego. Much too many pedantic questions and answers. Franny sounded as though she had a head cold. Zooey was in dreamy top form. The announcer had them off on the subject of housing developments, and the little Burke girl said she hated houses that all look alike – meaning a long row of identical 'development' houses. Zooey said they were "nice." He said it would be very nice to come home and be in the wrong house. To eat dinner with the wrong people by mistake, sleep in the wrong bed by mistake, and kiss everybody goodbye in the morning thinking they were your own family. He said he even wished everybody in the world looked exactly alike. He said you'd keep thinking everybody you met was your wife or your mother or father, and people would always be throwing their arms around each other wherever they went, and it would look "very nice."

'I felt unbearably happy all evening. The familiarity between Muriel and her mother struck me as being so beautiful when we were all sitting in the living room. They know each other's weaknesses, especially conversational weaknesses, and pick at them with their eyes. Mrs Fedder's eyes watch over Muriel's conversational taste in "literature," and Muriel's eyes watch over her mother's tendency to be windy, verbose. When they argue, there can be no danger of a permanent rift, because they're Mother and Daughter. A terrible and beautiful phenomenon to watch. Yet there are times when I sit there enchanted that I wish Mr Fedder were more conversationally active. Sometimes I feel I need him. Sometimes, in fact, when I come in the front door, it's like entering a kind of untidy, secular, two-woman convent. Sometimes when I leave, I have a peculiar feeling that both M. and her mother have stuffed my pockets with little bottles and tubes containing lipstick, rouge, hair nets, deodorants, and so on. I feel overwhelmingly grateful to them, but I don't know what to do with their invisible gifts.'

'We didn't get our passes directly after retreat this evening, because someone dropped his rifle while the visiting British general was making his inspection. I missed the 5:52 and was an hour late meeting Muriel. Dinner at Lun Far's on 58th. M. irritable and tearful throughout dinner, genuinely upset and scared. Her mother thinks I'm a schizoid personality. Apparently she's spoken to her psychoanalyst about me, and he agrees with her. Mrs Fedder has asked Muriel to find out discreetly if there's any insanity in the family. I gather that Muriel was naïve enough to tell her where I got the scars on my wrists, poor sweet baby. From what M. says, however, this doesn't bother her mother nearly so much as a couple of other things. Three other things. One, I withdraw from and fail to relate to people. Two, apparently there is something "wrong" with me because I haven't seduced Muriel. Three, evidently Mrs Fedder has been haunted for days by my remark at dinner one night that I'd like to be a dead cat. She asked me at dinner last week what I intended to do after I got out of the Army. Did I intend to resume teaching at the same college? Would I go back to teaching at all? Would I consider going back on the radio, possibly as a "commentator" of some kind? I answered that it seemed to me that the war might go on forever, and that I was only certain that if peace ever came again I would like to be a dead cat. Mrs Fedder thought I was cracking a joke of some kind. A sophisticated joke. She thinks I'm very sophisticated, according to Muriel. She thought my deadly-serious comment was the sort of joke one ought to acknowledge with a light, musical laugh. When she laughed, I suppose it distracted me a little, and I forgot to explain to her. I told Muriel tonight that in Zen Buddhism a master was once asked what was the most valuable thing in the world, and the master answered that a dead cat was, because no one could put a price on it. M. was relieved, but I could see she could hardly wait to get home to assure her mother of the harmlessness of my remark. She rode to the station with me in the cab. How sweet she was, and in so much better humor. She was trying to teach me to smile, spreading the muscles around my mouth with her fingers. How beautiful it is to see her laugh. Oh, God, I'm so happy with her. If only she could be happier with me. I amuse her at times, and she seems to like my face and hands and the back of my head, and she gets a vast satisfaction out of telling her friends that she's engaged to the Billy Black who was on "It's a Wise Child" for years. And I think she feels a mixed maternal and sexual drive in my general direction. But on the whole I don't make her really happy. Oh, God, help me. My one terrible consolation is that my beloved has an undying, basically undeviating love for the institution of marriage itself. She has a primal urge to play house permanently. Her marital goals are so absurd and touching. She wants to get a very dark sun tan and go up to the desk clerk in some very posh hotel and ask if her Husband has picked up the mail yet. She wants to shop for curtains. She wants to shop for maternity clothes. She wants to get out of her mother's house, whether she knows it or not, and despite her attachment to her. She wants children – good-looking children, with her features, not mine. I have a feeling, too, that she wants her own Christmas-tree ornaments to unbox annually, not her mother's.

'A very funny letter came from Buddy today, written just after he came off K.P. I think of him as I write about Muriel. He would despise her for her marriage motives as I've put them down here. But are they despicable? In a way, they must be, but yet they seem to me so human-size and beautiful that I can't think of them even now as I write this without feeling deeply, deeply moved. He would disapprove of Muriel's mother, too. She's an irritating, opinionated woman, a type Buddy can't stand. I don't think he could see her for what she is. A person deprived, for life, of any understanding or taste for the main current of poetry that flows through things, all things. She might as well be dead, and yet she goes on living, stopping off at delicatessens, seeing her analyst, consuming a novel every night, putting on her girdle, plotting for Muriel's health and prosperity. I love her. I find her unimaginably brave.'

'The whole company is restricted to the post tonight. Stood in line for a full hour to get to use the phone in the Rec Room. Muriel sounded rather relieved that I couldn't get in tonight. Which amuses and delights me. Another girl, if she genuinely wanted an evening free of her fiancé, would go through the motions of expressing regret over the phone. M. just said Oh when I told her. How I worship her simplicity, her terrible honesty. How I rely on it.'

'3:30 A.M. I'm over in the Orderly Room. I couldn't sleep. I put my coat on over my pajamas and came over here. Al Aspesi is C.Q. He's asleep on the floor. I can stay here if I answer the phone for him. What a night. Mrs Fedder's analyst was there for dinner and grilled me, off and on, till about eleven-thirty. Occasionally with great skill, intelligence. Once or twice, I found myself pulling for him. Apparently he's an old fan of Buddy's and mine. He seemed personally as well as professionally interested in why I'd been bounced off the show at sixteen. He'd actually heard the Lincoln broadcast, but he had the impression that I'd said over the air that the Gettysburg Address was "bad for children." Not true. I told him I'd said I thought it was a bad speech for children to have to memorize in school. He also had the impression I'd said it was a dishonest speech. I told him I'd said that 51,112 men were casualties at Gettysburg, and that if someone *had* to speak at the anniversary of the event, he should simply have come forward and shaken his fist at his audience and then walked off – that is, if the speaker was an absolutely honest man. He didn't disagree with me, but he seemed to feel that I have a perfection complex of some kind. Much talk from him, and quite intelligent, on the virtues of living the imperfect life, of accepting one's own and others' weaknesses. I agree with him, but only in theory. I'll champion indiscrimination till doomsday, on the ground that it leads to health and a kind of very real, enviable happiness. *Followed purely* it's the way of the Tao, and undoubtedly the highest way. But for a discriminating man to achieve this, it would mean that he would have to dispossess himself of poetry, go *beyond* poetry. That is, he couldn't possibly learn or drive himself to *like* bad poetry in the abstract, let alone equate it with good poetry. He would have to drop poetry altogether. I said it would be no easy thing to do. Dr Sims said I was putting it too stringently – putting it, he said, as only a perfectionist would. Can I deny that?

'Evidently Mrs Fedder had nervously told him about Charlotte's nine stitches. It was rash, I suppose, to have mentioned that old finished business to Muriel. She passes everything along to her mother while it's hot. I should object, no doubt, but I can't. M. can only hear me when her mother is listening, too, poor baby. But I had no intention of discussing Charlotte's stitches with Sims. Not over just one drink.

'I more or less promised M. at the station tonight that I'll go to a psychoanalyst one of these days. Sims told me that the man right here on the post is very good. Evidently he and Mrs Fedder have had a tête-à-tête or two on the subject. Why doesn't this rankle me? It doesn't. It seems funny. It warms me, for no good reason. Even stock mothers-in-law in the funny papers have always remotely appealed to me. Anyway, I can't see that I have anything to lose by seeing an analyst. If I do it in the Army, it'll be free. M. loves me, but she'll never feel really close to me, *familiar* with me, *frivolous* with me, till I'm slightly overhauled.

'If or when I do start going to an analyst, I hope to God he has the foresight to let a dermatologist sit in on consultation. A hand specialist. I have scars on my hands from touching certain people. Once, in the park, when Franny was still in the carriage, I put my hand on the downy pate of her head and left it there too long. Another time, at Loew's Seventy-second Street, with Zooey during a spooky movie. He was about six or seven, and he went under the seat to avoid watching a scary scene. I put my hand on his head. Certain heads, certain colors and textures of human hair leave permanent marks on me. Other things, too. Charlotte once ran away from me, outside the studio, and I grabbed her dress to stop her, to keep her near me. A yellow cotton dress I loved because it was too long for her. I still have a lemon-yellow mark on the palm of my right hand. Oh, God, if I'm anything by a clinical name, I'm a kind of paranoiac in reverse. I suspect people of plotting to make me happy.'

I remember closing the diary – actually, slamming it shut – after the word 'happy.' I then sat for several minutes with the diary under one arm, until I became conscious of a certain discomfort from having sat so long on the side of the bathtub. When I stood up, I found I was perspiring more profusely than I had all day, as though I had just got out of a tub, rather than just been sitting on the side of one. I went over to the laundry hamper, raised the lid, and, with an almost vicious wrist movement, literally threw Seymour's diary into some sheets and pillowcases that were on the bottom of the hamper. Then, for want of a better, more constructive idea, I went back and sat down on the side of the bathtub again. I stared for a minute or two at Boo Boo's message on the medicine-cabinet mirror, and then I left the bathroom, closing the door excessively hard after me, as though sheer force might lock up the place forever after.

My next stop was the kitchen. Fortunately, it led off the hall, and I could get there without having to go through the living room and face my guests. On arrival, and with the swinging door closed behind me, I took off my coat – my tunic – and dropped it across the enamel table. It seemed to require all my energy just to take off my coat, and I stood for some time, in my T shirt, just resting up, as it were, before taking on the herculean task of mixing drinks. Then, abruptly, as though I were being invisibly policed through small apertures in the wall, I began to open cabinet and refrigerator doors, looking for Tom Collins ingredients. They were all there, except for lemons instead of limes, and in a few minutes I had a somewhat sugary pitcherful of Collinses made. I took down five glasses, and then looked around for a tray. It was just hard enough to find a tray, and it took me just long enough, so that by the time I did find one, I was giving out small, faintly audible whimpers as I opened and shut cabinet doors.

Just as I was starting out of the kitchen, with the pitcher and glasses loaded on the tray, and with my coat back on, an imaginary light bulb was turned on over my head – the way it is in comic strips to show that a character has a sudden very bright idea. I put down the tray on the floor. I went back over to the liquor shelf and took down a half-full fifth of Scotch. I brought my glass over and poured myself out – somewhat accidentally – at least four fingers of Scotch. I looked at the glass critically for a split second, and then, like a tried-and-true leading man in a Western movie, drank it off in one deadpan toss. A little piece of business, I might well mention, that I record here with a rather distinct shudder. Granted that I was twenty-three, and that I may have been doing only what any red-blooded twenty-three-year-old simpleton would have done under similar circumstances. I don't mean anything quite so simple as that. I mean that I am Not a Drinker, as the expression goes. On an ounce of whiskey, as a rule, I either get violently sick or I start scanning the room for unbelievers. On two ounces I've been known to pass out cold.

This was, however – by way of an unparalleled understatement – no ordinary day, and I remember that as I picked up the tray again and started to leave the kitchen, I felt none of the usual almost immediate metamorphic changes. There seemed to be an unprecedented degree of heat being generated in the subject's stomach, but that was all.

In the living room, as I brought in the loaded tray, there were no auspicious changes in the deportment of my guests, beyond the revitalizing fact that the bride's father's uncle had rejoined the group. He was ensconced in my dead Boston bull's old chair. His tiny legs were crossed, his hair was combed, his gravy stain was as arresting as ever, and – lo and behold – *his cigar was lighted*. We greeted each other even more extravagantly than usual, as though these intermittent separations were suddenly too long and unnecessary for either of us to bear with.

The Lieutenant was still over at the bookshelves. He stood turning the pages of a book he'd taken out, apparently engrossed in it. (I never did find out which book it was.) Mrs Silsburn, looking considerably pulled together, even refreshed, with her pancake makeup, I thought, newly attended to, was seated on the couch now, in the corner of it farthest away from the bride's father's uncle. She was leafing through a magazine. 'Oh, how lovely!' she said, in a party voice, as she sighted the tray I'd just put down on the coffee table. She smiled up at me convivially.

'I've put very little gin in it,' I lied as I began to stir the pitcher.

'It's so lovely and cool in here now,' Mrs Silsburn said. 'May I ask you a question, incidentally?' With that, she put aside her magazine, got up, and crossed around the couch and over to the desk. She reached up and placed a fingertip on one of the photographs on the wall. '*Who* is this beautiful child?' she asked me. With the air-conditioner now smoothly and steadily in operation, and having had time to apply fresh makeup, she was no longer the wilted, timorous child who had stood in the hot sun outside Schrafft's Seventy-ninth Street. She was addressing me now with all the brittle equipoise that had been at her disposal when I first jumped into the car, outside the bride's grandmother's house, when she asked me if I was someone named Dickie Briganza.

I left off stirring the pitcher of Collinses, and went around and over to her. She had fixed a lacquered fingernail on the photograph of the 1929 cast of 'It's a Wise Child,' and on one child in particular. Seven of us were sitting around a circular table, a microphone in front of each child. 'That's the most beautiful child I've ever laid *eyes* on,' Mrs Silsburn said. 'You know who she looks a teeny bit like? Around the eyes and mouth?'

At about that point, some of the Scotch – roughly, a finger of it, I'd say – was beginning to affect me, and I very nearly answered, 'Dickie Briganza,' but a certain cautionary impulse still prevailed. I nodded, and said the name of the motion-picture actress whom the Matron of Honor, earlier in the afternoon, had mentioned in connection with nine surgical stitches.

Mrs Silsburn stared at me. 'Was *she* on "It's a Wise Child"?' she asked.

'For about two years, yes. God, yes. Under her own name, of course. Charlotte Mayhew.'

The Lieutenant was now behind me, at my right, looking up at the photograph. At the drop of Charlotte's professional name, he had stepped over from the bookshelves to have a look.

'I didn't know she was ever on the radio as a child!' Mrs Silsburn said. 'I didn't know that! Was she so brilliant as a child?'

'No, she was mostly just noisy, really. She sang as well then as she does now, though. And she was wonderful moral support. She usually arranged things so that she sat next to my brother Seymour at the broadcasting table, and whenever he said anything on the show that delighted her, she used to step on his foot. It was like a hand squeeze, only she used her foot.' As I delivered this little homily, I had my hands on the top rung of the straight chair at the desk. They suddenly slipped off – rather in the way one's elbow can abruptly lose its 'footing' on the surface of a table or a bar counter. I lost and regained my balance almost simultaneously, though, and neither Mrs Silsburn nor the Lieutenant seemed to notice it. I folded my arms. 'On certain nights when he was in especially good form, Seymour used to come home with a slight limp. That's really true. Charlotte didn't just step on his foot, she tramped on it. He didn't care. He loved people who stepped on his feet. He loved noisy girls.'

'Well, isn't that interesting!' Mrs Silsburn said. 'I *cer*tainly never knew she was ever on the radio or anything.'

'Seymour got her on, actually,' I said. 'She was the daughter of an osteopath who lived in our building on Riverside Drive.' I replaced my hands on the rung of the straight chair, and leaned my weight forward on it, partly for support, partly in the style of an old back-fence reminiscer. The sound of my own voice was now singularly pleasing to me. 'We were playing stoopball – Are either of you at all interested in this?'

'Yes!' said Mrs Silsburn.

'We were playing stoopball on the side of the building one afternoon after school, Seymour and I, and somebody who turned out to be Charlotte started dropping marbles on us from the twelfth story. That's how we met. We got her on the program that same week. We didn't even know she could sing. We just wanted her because she had such a beautiful New Yorkese accent. She had a Dyckman Street accent.'

Mrs Silsburn laughed the kind of tinkling laugh that is, of course, death to the sensitive anecdotist, cold sober or otherwise. She had evidently been waiting for me to finish, so that she could make a single-minded appeal to the Lieutenant. 'Who does she look like to you?' she said to him importunately. 'Around the eyes and mouth especially. Who does she remind you of?'

The Lieutenant looked at her, then up at the photograph. 'You mean the way she is in this picture? As a kid?' he said. 'Or now? The way she is in the movies? Which do you mean?'

'Both, really, *I* think. But especially right here in this picture.'

The Lieutenant scrutinized the photograph – rather severely, I thought, as though he by no means approved of the way Mrs Silsburn, who after all was a civilian as well as a woman, had asked him to examine it. 'Muriel,' he said shortly. 'Looks like Muriel in this picture. The hair and all.'

'But exactly!' said Mrs Silsburn. She turned to me. 'But *exactly*,' she repeated. 'Have you ever met Muriel? I mean have you ever seen her when she's had her hair tied in a lovely big –'

'I've never seen Muriel at all until today,' I said.

'Well, all right, just take my word.' Mrs Silsburn tapped the photograph impressively with her index finger. 'This child could *double* for Muriel at that age. But to a T.'

The whiskey was steadily edging up on me, and I couldn't quite take in this information whole, let alone consider its many possible ramifications. I walked back over – just a trifle straight-linishly, I think – to the coffee table and resumed stirring the pitcher of Collinses. The bride's father's uncle tried to get my attention as I came back into his vicinity, to greet me on my reappearance, but I was just abstracted enough by the alleged fact of Muriel's resemblance to Charlotte not to respond to him. I was also feeling just a trifle dizzy. I had a strong impulse, which I didn't indulge, to stir the pitcher from a seated position on the floor.

A minute or two later, as I was just starting to pour out the drinks, Mrs Silsburn had a question for me. It all but sang its way across the room to me, so melodiously was it pitched. 'Would it be very awful if I asked about that accident Mrs Burwick happened to mention before? I mean those nine stitches she spoke of. Did your brother accidentally *push* her or something like that, I mean?'

I put down the pitcher, which seemed extraordinarily heavy and unwieldy, and looked over at her. Oddly, despite the mild dizziness I was feeling, distant images hadn't begun to blur in the least. If anything, Mrs Silsburn as a focal point across the room seemed rather obtrusively distinct. 'Who's Mrs Burwick?' I said.

'My wife,' the Lieutenant answered, a trifle shortly. He was looking over at me, too, if only as a committee of one to investigate what was taking me so long with the drinks.

'Oh. Certainly she is,' I said.

'Was it an accident?' Mrs Silsburn pressed. 'He didn't *mean* to do it, did he?'

'Oh, *God*, Mrs Silsburn.'

'I beg your pardon?' she said coldly.

'I'm sorry. Don't pay any attention to me. I'm getting a little tight. I poured myself a great drink in the kitchen about five minutes –' I broke off, and turned abruptly around. I'd just heard a familiar heavy tread in the uncarpeted hall. It was coming toward us – at us – at a great rate, and in an instant the Matron of Honor jounced into the room.

She had eyes for no one. 'I finally got them,' she said. Her voice sounded strangely levelled off, stripped of even the ghost of italics. 'After about an hour.' Her face looked tense and overheated to the bursting point. 'Is that cold?' she said, and came without stopping, and unanswered, over to the coffee table. She picked up the one glass I'd half filled a minute or so before, and drank it off in one greedy tilt. 'That's the hottest room I've ever been in in my entire life,' she said – rather impersonally – and set down her empty glass. She picked up the pitcher and refilled the glass halfway, with much clinking and plopping of ice cubes.

Mrs Silsburn was already well in the vicinity of the coffee table. 'What'd they say?' she asked impatiently. 'Did you speak to Rhea?'

The Matron of Honor drank first. 'I spoke to everybody,' she said, putting down her glass, and with a grim but, for her, peculiarly undramatic emphasis on 'everybody.' She looked first at Mrs Silsburn, then at me, then at the Lieutenant. 'You can all relax,' she said. 'Everything's just fine and dandy.'

'What do you mean? What happened?' Mrs Silsburn said sharply.

'Just what I said. The *groom's* no longer indis*posed* by *hap*piness.' A familiar style of inflection was back in the Matron of Honor's voice.

'How come? Who'd you talk to?' the Lieutenant said to her. 'Did you talk to Mrs Fedder?'

'I said I talked to everybody. Everybody but the blushing bride. She and the groom've eloped.' She turned to me. 'How much sugar did you put in this thing, anyway?' she asked irritably. 'It tastes like absolute –'

'*Eloped?*' said Mrs Silsburn, and put her hand to her throat.

The Matron of Honor looked at her. 'All right, just relax now,' she advised. 'You'll live longer.'

Mrs Silsburn sat down inertly on the couch – right beside me, as a matter of fact. I was staring up at the Matron of Honor, and I'm sure Mrs Silsburn immediately followed suit.

'Apparently he was *at* the apartment when they got back. So Muriel just ups and packs her bag, and off the two of them go, just like that.' The Matron of Honor shrugged her shoulders elaborately. She picked up her glass again and finished her drink. 'Anyway, we're all invited to the reception. Or whatever you call it when the bride and groom have already *left*. From what I gathered, there's a whole mob of people over there already. Everybody sounded so *gay* on the phone.'

'You said you talked to Mrs Fedder. What'd she say?' the Lieutenant said.

The Matron of Honor shook her head, rather cryptically. 'She was wonderful. My God, what a woman. She sounded absolutely normal. From what I gathered – I mean from what she said – this *Sey*mour's promised to start going to an analyst and get himself straightened out.' She shrugged her shoulders again. 'Who knows?

Maybe everything's gonna be hunky-dory. I'm too pooped to think any more.' She looked at her husband. 'Let's go. Where's your little hat?'

The next thing I knew, the Matron of Honor, the Lieutenant, and Mrs Silsburn were all filing toward the front door, with me, as their host, following behind them. I was weaving now very obviously, but since no one turned around, I think my condition went unnoticed.

I heard Mrs Silsburn say to the Matron of Honor, 'Are you going to stop by there, or what?'

'I don't know,' came the reply. 'If we do, it'll just be for a minute.'

The Lieutenant rang the elevator bell, and the three stood leadenly watching the indicator dial. No one seemed to have any further use for speech. I stood in the doorway of the apartment, a few feet away, dimly looking on. When the elevator door opened, I said goodbye, aloud, and their three heads turned in unison toward me. 'Oh, good*bye*,' they called over, and I heard the Matron of Honor shout 'Thanks for the drink!' as the elevator door closed behind them.

I went back into the apartment, very unsteadily, trying to unbutton my tunic as I wandered along, or to yank it open.

My return to the living room was unreservedly hailed by my one remaining guest – whom I'd forgotten. He raised a well-filled glass at me as I came into the room. In fact, he literally waved it at me, wagging his head up and down and grinning, as though the supreme, jubilant moment we had both been long awaiting had finally arrived. I found I couldn't quite match grins with him at this particular reunion. I remember patting him on the shoulder, though. Then I went over and sat down heavily on the couch, directly opposite him, and finished yanking open my coat. 'Don't you have a home to go to?' I asked him. 'Who looks after you? The pigeons in the park?' In response to these provocative questions, my guest toasted me with increased gusto, wielding his Tom Collins at me as though it were a beer stein. I closed my eyes and lay back on the couch, putting my feet up and stretching out flat. But this made the room spin. I sat up and swung my feet around to the floor – doing it so suddenly and with such poor coordination that I had to put my hand on the coffee table to keep my balance. I sat slumped forward for a minute or two, with my eyes closed. Then, without having to get up, I reached for the Tom Collins pitcher and poured myself out a drink, spilling any amount of liquid and ice cubes onto the table and floor. I sat with the filled glass in my hands for some more minutes, without drinking, and then I put it down in a shallow puddle on the coffee table. 'Would you like to know how Charlotte got those nine stitches?' I asked suddenly, in a tone of voice that sounded perfectly normal to me. 'We were up at the Lake. Seymour had written to Charlotte, inviting her to come up and visit us, and her mother finally let her. What happened was, she sat down in the middle of our driveway one morning to pet Boo Boo's cat, and Seymour threw a stone at her. He was twelve. That's all there was to it. He threw it at her because she looked so beautiful sitting there in the middle of the driveway with Boo Boo's cat. Everybody knew that, for God's sake – me, Charlotte, Boo Boo, Waker, Walt, the whole family.' I stared at the pewter ashtray on the coffee table. 'Charlotte never said a word to him about it. Not a word.' I looked up at my guest, rather expecting him to dispute me, to call me a liar. I am a liar, of course. Charlotte never did understand why Seymour threw that stone at her. My guest didn't dispute me, though. The contrary. He grinned at me encouragingly, as though anything further I had to say on the subject could go down only as the absolute truth with him. I got up, though, and left the room. I remember considering, halfway across the room, going back and picking up two ice cubes that were on the floor, but it seemed too arduous an undertaking, and I continued along to the hall. As I passed the kitchen door, I took off my tunic – peeled it off – and dropped it on the floor. It seemed, at the time, like the place where I always left my coat.

In the bathroom, I stood for several minutes over the laundry hamper, debating whether I should or shouldn't take out Seymour's diary and look at it again. I don't remember any more what arguments I advanced on the subject, either pro or con, but I did finally open the hamper and pick out the diary. I sat down with it, on the side of the bathtub again, and riffled the pages till I came to the very last entry Seymour had made:

'One of the men just called the flight line again. If the ceiling keeps lifting, apparently we can get off before morning. Oppenheim says not to hold our breaths. I phoned Muriel to tell her. It was very strange. She answered the phone and kept saying hello. My voice wouldn't work. She very nearly hung up. If only I could calm down a little. Oppenheim is going to hit the sack till the flight line calls us back. I should, too, but I'm too keyed up. I really called to ask her, to beg her for the last time to just go off alone with me and get married. I'm too keyed up to be with people. I feel as though I'm about to be born. Sacred, sacred day. The connection was so bad, and I couldn't talk at all during most of the call. How terrible it is when you say I love you and the person at the other end shouts back "What?" I've been reading a miscellany of Vedanta all day. Marriage partners are to serve each other. Elevate, help, teach, strengthen each other, but above all, *serve*. Raise their children honorably, lovingly, and with detachment. A child is a guest in the house, to be loved and respected – never possessed, since he belongs to God. How wonderful, how sane, how beautifully difficult, and therefore true. The joy of responsibility for the first time in my life. Oppenheim is already in the sack. I should be, too, but I can't. Someone must sit up with the happy man.'

I read the entry through just once, then closed the diary and brought it back to the bedroom with me. I dropped it into Seymour's canvas bag, on the window seat. Then I fell, more or less deliberately, on the nearer of the two beds. I was asleep – or, possibly, out cold – before I landed, or so it seemed.

When I wakened, about an hour and a half later, I had a splitting headache and a parched mouth. The room was all but dark. I remember sitting for rather a long time on the edge of the bed. Then, in the cause of a great thirst, I got up and gravitated slowly toward the living room, hoping there were still some cold and wet remnants in the pitcher on the coffee table.

My last guest had evidently let himself out of the apartment. Only his empty glass, and his cigar end in the pewter ashtray, indicated that he had ever existed. I still rather think his cigar end should have been forwarded on to Seymour, the usual run of wedding gifts being what it is. Just the cigar, in a small, nice box. Possibly with a blank sheet of paper enclosed, by way of explanation.

SEYMOUR–
AN INTRODUCTION

> The actors by their presence always convince me, to my horror, that most of what I've written about them until now is false. It is false because I write about them with steadfast love (even now, while I write it down, this, too, becomes false) but varying ability, and this varying ability does not hit off the real actors loudly and correctly but loses itself dully in this love that will never be satisfied with the ability and therefore thinks it is protecting the actors by preventing this ability from exercising itself.
>
> It is (to describe it figuratively) as if an author were to make a slip of the pen, and as if this clerical error became conscious of being such. Perhaps this was no error but in a far higher sense was an essential part of the whole exposition. It is, then, as if this clerical error were to revolt against the author, out of hatred for him, were to forbid him to correct it, and were to say, 'No, I will not be erased, I will stand as a witness against thee, that thou art a very poor writer.'

At times, frankly, I find it pretty slim pickings, but at the age of forty I look on my old fair-weather friend the general reader as my last deeply contemporary confidant, and I was rather strenuously requested, long before I was out of my teens, by at once the most exciting and the least fundamentally bumptious public craftsman I've ever personally known, to try to keep a steady and sober regard for the amenities of such a relationship, be it ever so peculiar or terrible; in my case, he saw it coming on from the first. The question is, how can a writer observe the amenities if he has no idea what his general reader is like? The reverse is common enough, most certainly, but just when is the author of a story ever asked what he thinks the reader is like? Very luckily, to push on and make my point here – and I don't think it's the kind of point that will survive an interminable buildup – I found out a good many years back practically all I need to know about *my* general reader; that is to say, *you*, I'm afraid. You'll deny it up and down, I fear, but I'm really in no position to take your word for it. You're a great bird-lover. Much like a man in a short story called 'Skule Skerry,' by John Buchan, which Arnold L. Sugarman, Jr, once pressed me to read during a very poorly supervised study-hall period, you're someone who took up birds in the first place because they fired your imagination; they fascinated you because 'they seemed of all created beings the nearest to pure spirit – those little creatures with a normal temperature of 125°.' Probably just like this John Buchan man, you thought many thrilling related thoughts; you reminded yourself, I don't doubt, that: 'The gold-crest, with a stomach no bigger than a bean, flies across the North Sea! The curlew sandpiper, which breeds so far north that only about three people have ever seen its nest, goes to Tasmania for its holidays!' It would be too much of a good thing to hope, of course, that my very own general reader should turn out to be one of the three people who have actually seen the curlew sandpiper's nest, but I feel, at least, that I know him – you – quite well enough to guess what kind of well-meant gesture might be welcomed from me right now. In this *entre-nous* spirit, then, old confidant, before we join the others, the grounded everywhere, including, I'm sure, the middle-aged hot-rodders who insist on zooming us to the moon, the Dharma Bums, the makers of cigarette filters for thinking men, the Beat and the Sloppy and the Petulant, the chosen cultists, all the lofty experts who know so well what we should or shouldn't do with our poor little sex organs, all the bearded, proud, unlettered young men and unskilled guitarists and Zen-killers and incorporated aesthetic Teddy boys who look down their thoroughly unenlightened noses at this splendid planet where (please don't shut me up) Kilroy, Christ, and Shakespeare all stopped – before we join these others, I privately say to you, old friend (unto you, really, I'm afraid), please accept from me this unpretentious bouquet of very early-blooming parentheses: (((()))). I suppose, most unflorally, I truly mean them to be taken, first off, as bowlegged – buckle-legged – omens of my state of mind and body at this writing.

Professionally speaking, which is the only way I've ever really enjoyed speaking up (and, just to ingratiate myself still less, I speak nine languages, incessantly, four of them stone-dead) – professionally speaking, I repeat, I'm an ecstatically happy man. I've never been before. Oh, once, perhaps, when I was fourteen and wrote a story in which all the characters had Heidelberg duelling scars – the hero, the villain, the heroine, her old nanny, all the horses and dogs. I was *rea*sonably happy then, you might say, but not ecstatically, not like this. To the point: I happen to know, possibly none better, that an ecstatically happy writing person is often a totally draining type to have around. Of course, the poets in this state are by far the most 'difficult,' but even the prose writer similarly seized hasn't any real choice of behavior in decent company; divine or not, a seizure's a seizure. And while I think an ecstatically happy prose writer can do many good things on the printed page – the best things, I'm frankly hoping – it's also true, and infinitely more self-evident, I suspect, that he can't be moderate or temperate or brief; he loses very nearly all his short paragraphs. He can't be detached – or only very rarely and suspiciously, on down-waves. In the wake of anything as large and consuming as happiness, he necessarily forfeits the much smaller but, for a writer, always rather exquisite pleasure of appearing on the page serenely sitting on a fence. Worst of all, I think, he's no longer in a position to look after the reader's most immediate want; namely, to see the author get the hell on with his story. Hence, in part, that ominous offering of parentheses a few sentences back. I'm aware that a good many perfectly intelligent people can't stand parenthetical comments while a story's purportedly being told. (We're advised of these things by mail – mostly, granted, by thesis preparers with very natural, oaty urges to write us under the table in their off-campus time. But we read, and usually we believe; good, bad, or indifferent, any string of English words holds our attention as if it came from Prospero himself.) I'm here to advise that not only will my asides run rampant from this point on (I'm not sure, in fact, that there won't be a footnote or two) but I fully intend, from time to time, to jump up personally on the reader's back when I see something off the beaten plot line that looks exciting or interesting and worth steering toward. Speed, here, God save my American hide, means nothing whatever to me. There are, however, readers who seriously require only the most restrained, most classical, and possibly deftest methods of having their attention drawn, and I suggest – as honestly as a writer can suggest this sort of thing – that they leave now, while, I can imagine, the leaving's good and easy. I'll probably continue to point out available exits as we move along, but I'm not sure I'll pretend to put my heart into it again.

I'd like to start out with some rather unstinting words about those two opening quotations. 'The actors by their presence . . .' is from Kafka. The second one – 'It is (to describe it figuratively) as if an author were to make a slip of the pen . . .' – is from Kierkegaard (and it's all I can do to keep from unattractively rubbing my hands together at the thought that this particular Kierkegaard passage may catch a few Existentialists and somewhat overpublished French mandarins with their – well, by some little surprise).* I don't really deeply feel that anyone needs an airtight reason for quoting from the works of writers he loves, but it's always nice, I'll grant you, if he has one. In this case, it seems to me that those two passages, especially in contiguity, are wonderfully representative of the best, in a sense, not only of Kafka and Kierkegaard but of all the four dead men, the four variously notorious Sick Men or underadjusted bachelors (probably only van Gogh, of the four, will be excused from making a guest appearance in these pages), whom I most often run to – occasionally in real distress – when I want any perfectly credible information about modern artistic processes. By and large, I've reproduced the two passages to try to suggest very plainly how I think I stand in regard to the overall mass of data I hope to assemble here – a thing that in some quarters, I don't a bit mind saying, an author can't be too explicit about, or any too early. In part, though, it

* This modest aspersion is *thoroughly* reprehensible, but the fact that the great Kierkegaard was never a Kierkegaardian, let alone an Existentialist, cheers one bush-league intellectual's heart no end, never fails to reaffirm his faith in a cosmic poetic justice, if not a cosmic Santa Claus.

would be rewarding for me to think, to dream, that those two short quotations may quite conceivably serve as a sort of spot convenience to the comparatively new breed of literary critics – the many workers (soldiers, I suppose you *could* say) who put in long hours, often with waning hopes of distinction, in our busy neo-Freudian Arts and Letters clinics. Especially, perhaps, those still very young students and greener clinicians, themselves implicitly bursting with good mental health, themselves (undeniably, I think) free of any inherent morbid *attrait* to beauty, who one day intend to specialize in aesthetic pathology. (Admittedly, this is a subject I've felt flinty about since I was eleven years old and watched the artist and Sick Man I've loved most in this world, then still in knee pants, being examined by a reputable group of professional Freudians for six hours and forty-five minutes. In my not altogether reliable opinion, they stopped just short of taking a brain smear from him, and I've had an idea for years that only the latish hour – 2 A.M. – dissuaded them from doing exactly that. Flinty, then, I do indeed mean to sound here. Churlish, no. I can perceive, though, that it's a very thin line, or plank, but I'd like to try to walk it for a minute more; ready or not, I've waited a good many years to collect these sentiments and get them off.) A great variety of rumors, of course, run high and wide about the extraordinarily, the sensationally creative artist – and I'm alluding exclusively, here, to painters and poets and full *Dichter*. One of these rumors – and by far, to me, the most exhilarating of the lot – is that he has never, even in the pre-psychoanalytical dark ages, deeply venerated his professional critics, and has, in fact, usually lumped them, in his generally unsound views of society, with the *echt* publishers and art dealers and the other, perhaps enviably prosperous camp followers of the arts who, he's just scarcely said to concede, would prefer different, possibly cleaner work if they could get it. But what, at least in modern times, I think one most recurrently hears about the curiously-productive-though-ailing poet or painter is that he is invariably a kind of super-size but unmistakably 'classical' neurotic, an aberrant who only occasionally, and never deeply, wishes to surrender his aberration; or, in English, a Sick Man who not at all seldom, though he's reported to childishly deny it, gives out terrible cries of pain, as if he would wholeheartedly let go both his art and his soul to experience what passes in other people for wellness, and yet (the rumor continues) when his unsalutary-looking little room is broken into and someone – not infrequently, at that, someone who actually loves him – passionately asks him where the pain is, he either declines or seems unable to discuss it at any constructive clinical length, and in the morning, when even great poets and painters presumably feel a bit more chipper than usual, he looks more perversely determined than ever to see his sickness run its course, as though by the light of another, presumably *working* day he had remembered that all men, the healthy ones included, eventually die, and usually with a certain amount of bad grace, but that *he*, lucky man, is at least being done in by the most stimulating companion, disease or no, he has ever known. On the whole, treacherous as it may sound, coming from me, with just such a dead artist in the immediate family as I've been alluding to throughout this near-polemic, I don't see how one can rationally deduce that this last general rumor (and mouthful) isn't based on a fairish amount of substantial fact. While my distinguished relative lived, I watched him – almost literally, I sometimes think – like a hawk. By every logical definition, he *was* an unhealthy specimen, he *did* on his worst nights and late afternoons give out not only cries of pain but cries for help, and when nominal help arrived, he *did* decline to say in perfectly intelligible language where it hurt. Even so, I do openly cavil with the declared experts in these matters – the scholars, the biographers, and especially the current ruling intellectual aristocracy educated in one or another of the big public psychoanalytical schools – and I cavil with them most acrimoniously over *this*: they don't listen properly to cries of pain when they come. They can't, of course. They're a peerage of tin ears. With such faulty equipment, with *those* ears, how can anyone possibly trace the pain, by sound and quality alone, back to its source? With such wretched hearing equipment, the best, I think, that can be detected, and perhaps verified, is a few stray, thin overtones – hardly even counterpoint – coming from a troubled childhood or a disordered libido. But where does by far the bulk, the whole ambulance load, of pain really come from? Where *must* it come from? Isn't the true poet or painter a seer? Isn't he, actually, the only seer we have on earth? Most apparently not the scientist, most emphatically not the psychiatrist. (Surely the one and only great poet the psychoanalysts have had was Freud himself; he had a little ear trouble of his own, no doubt, but who in his right mind could deny that an epic poet was at work?) Forgive me; I'm nearly finished with this. In a seer, what part of the human anatomy would necessarily be required to take the most abuse? The *eyes*, certainly. Please, dear general reader, as a last indulgence (if you're still here), reread those two short passages from Kafka and Kierkegaard I started out with. Isn't it *clear*? Don't those cries come straight from the eyes? However contradictory the coroner's report – whether he pronounces Consumption or Loneliness or Suicide to be the cause of death – isn't it plain how the true artist-seer actually dies? I say (and everything that follows in these pages all too possibly stands or falls on my being at least *nearly* right) – I say that the true artist-seer, the heavenly fool who can and does produce beauty, is mainly dazzled to death by his own scruples, the blinding shapes and colors of his own sacred human conscience.

My credo is stated. I sit back. I sigh – happily, I'm afraid. I light a Murad, and go on, I hope to God, to other things.

Something, now – and briskly, if I can – about that subtitle, 'An Introduction,' up near the top of the marquee. My central character here, at least in those lucid intervals when I can prevail upon myself to sit down and be reasonably quiet, will be my late, eldest brother, Seymour Glass, who (and I think I'd prefer to say this in one obituary-like sentence), in 1948, at the age of thirty-one, while vacationing down in Florida with his wife, committed suicide. He was a great many things to a great many people while he lived, and virtually all things to his brothers and sisters in our somewhat outsized family. Surely he was all *real* things to us: our blue-striped unicorn, our double-lensed burning glass, our consultant genius, our portable conscience, our supercargo, and our one full poet, and, inevitably, I think, since not only was reticence never his strongest suit but he spent nearly seven years of his childhood as star turn on a children's coast-to-coast radio quiz program, so there wasn't much that didn't eventually get aired, one way or another – inevitably, I think, he was also our rather notorious 'mystic' and 'unbalanced type.' And since I'm obviously going whole hog right here at the outset, I'll further enunciate – if one can enunciate and shout at the same time – that, with or without a suicide plot in his head, he was the only person I've ever habitually consorted with, banged around with, who more frequently than not tallied with the classical conception, as I saw it, of a *mukta*, a ringding enlightened man, a God-knower. At any rate, his character lends itself to no legitimate sort of narrative compactness that *I* know of, and I can't conceive of anyone, least of all myself, trying to write him off in one shot or in one fairly simple series of sittings, whether arranged by the month or the year. I come to the point: My original plans for this general space were to write a short story about Seymour and to call it 'SEYMOUR ONE,' with the big 'ONE' serving as a built-in convenience to me, Buddy Glass, even more than to the reader – a helpful, flashy reminder that other stories (a Seymour Two, Three, and possibly Four) would logically have to follow. Those plans no longer exist. Or, if they do – and I suspect that this is much more likely how things stand – they've gone underground, with an understanding, perhaps, that I'll rap three times when I'm ready. But on this occasion I'm anything but a short-story writer where my brother is concerned. What I *am*, I think, is a thesaurus of undetached prefatory remarks about him. I believe I essentially remain what I've almost always been – a narrator, but one with extremely pressing personal needs. I want to introduce, I want to describe, I want to distribute mementos, amulets, I want to break out my wallet and pass around snapshots, I want to follow my nose. In this mood, I don't dare go anywhere near the short-story form. It eats up fat little undetached writers like me whole.

But I have many, many unfelicitous-sounding things to tell you. For instance, I'm saying, cataloguing, so much so early about my brother. I feel you *must* have noticed. You may also have noticed – I know it hasn't entirely escaped *my* attention – that everything

I've so far said about Seymour (and about his blood type in general, as it were) has been graphically panegyric. It gives me pause, all right. Granted that I haven't come to bury but to exhume and, most likely, to praise, I nonetheless suspect that the honor of cool, dispassionate narrators everywhere is remotely at stake here. *Had* Seymour no grievous faults, no vices, no meannesses, that can be listed, at least in a hurry? What was he, anyway? A *saint*?

Thankfully, it isn't my responsibility to answer that one. (Oh, lucky day!) Let me change the subject and say, without hesitation, he had a Heinzlike variety of personal characteristics that threatened, at different chronological intervals of sensitivity or thin-skinnedness, to drive every minor in the family to the bottle. In the first place, there is very evidently one rather terrible hallmark common to all persons who look for God, and apparently with enormous success, in the queerest imaginable places – e.g., in radio announcers, in newspapers, in taxicabs with crooked meters, literally everywhere. (My brother, for the record, had a distracting habit, most of his adult life, of investigating loaded ashtrays with his index finger, clearing all the cigarette ends to the sides – smiling from ear to ear as he did it – as if he expected to see Christ himself curled up cherubically in the middle, and he never looked disappointed.) The hallmark, then, of the advanced religious, nonsectarian or any other (and I graciously include in the definition of an 'advanced religious,' odious though the phrase is, all Christians on the great Vivekananda's terms; i.e., 'See Christ, then you are a Christian; all else is talk') – the hallmark most commonly identifying this person is that he very frequently behaves like a fool, even an imbecile. It's a trial to a family that has a real grandee in it if he can't always be relied on to behave like one. I'm now about to quit cataloguing, but I can't do so quite at this point without citing what I think was his most trying personal characteristic. It had to do with his speech habits – or, rather, the anomalous range of his speech habits. Vocally, he was either as brief as a gatekeeper at a Trappist monastery – sometimes for days, weeks at a stretch – or he was a non-stop talker. When he was wound up (and, to state the matter exactly, almost everybody was forever winding him up, and then, of course, quickly sitting in close, the better to pick his brains) – when he was wound up, it was nothing for him to talk for hours at a time, occasionally with no redeeming awareness whatever that one or two or ten other people were in the room. He was an inspired non-stop talker, I'm firmly suggesting, but, to put it *very* mildly, even the most sublimely accomplished non-stop talker can't consistently please. And I say that, I should add, less from any repellent splendid impulse to play 'fair' with my invisible reader than – much worse, I suppose – because I believe that this particular non-stop talker can take almost any amount of knocking. Certainly from me, at any rate. I'm in the unique position of being able to call my brother, straight out, a *non-stop talker* – which is a pretty vile thing to call somebody, I think – and yet at the same time to sit back, rather, I'm afraid, like a type with both sleeves full of aces, and effortlessly remember a whole legion of mitigating factors (and 'mitigating' is hardly the word for it). I can condense them all into one: By the time Seymour was in mid-adolescence – sixteen, seventeen – he not only had learned to control his native vernacular, his many, many less than élite New York speech mannerisms, but had by then already come into his own true, bull's-eye, poet's vocabulary. His non-stop talks, his monologues, his near-harangues then came as close to pleasing from start to finish – for a good many of us, anyway – as, say, the bulk of Beethoven's output after he ceased being encumbered with a sense of hearing, and maybe I'm thinking especially, though it seems a trifle picky, of the B-flat-major and C-sharp-minor quartets. Still, we were a family of seven children, originally. And, as it happened, none of us was in the least tongue-tied. It's an exceedingly weighty matter when six naturally profuse verbalizers and expounders have an undefeatable champion talker in the house. True, he never sought the title. And he passionately yearned to see one or another of us outpoint or simply outlast him in a conversation or an argument. A small matter which, of course, though he himself never saw it – he had his blank spots, like everybody else – bothered some of us all the more. The fact remains that the title was always his, and though I think he would have given almost anything on earth to retire it – this is the weightiest matter of all, surely, and I'm not going to be able to explore it deeply for another few years – he never did find a completely graceful way of doing it.

At this point, it doesn't seem to me merely chummy to mention that I've written about my brother before. For that matter, with a little good-humored cajoling I might conceivably admit that there's seldom been a time when I haven't written about him, and if, presumably at gunpoint, I had to sit down tomorrow and write a story about a dinosaur, I don't doubt that I'd inadvertently give the big chap one or two small mannerisms reminiscent of Seymour – a singularly endearing way of biting off the top of a hemlock, say, or of wagging his thirty-foot tail. Some people – *not* close friends – have asked me whether a lot of Seymour didn't go into the young leading character of the one novel I've published. Actually, most of these people haven't *asked* me; they've *told* me. To protest this at all, I've found, makes me break out in hives, but I will say that no one who knew my brother has asked me or told me anything of the kind – for which I'm grateful, and, in a way, more than a bit impressed, since a good many of my main characters speak Manhattanese fluently and idiomatically, have a rather common flair for rushing in where most damned fools fear to tread, and are, by and large, pursued by an Entity that I'd much prefer to identify, very roughly, as the Old Man of the Mountain. But what I can and should state is that I've written and published two short stories that were supposed to be directly about Seymour. The more recent of the two, published in 1955, was a highly inclusive recount of his wedding day in 1942. The details were served up with a fullness possibly just short of presenting the reader with a sherbet mold of each and every wedding guest's footprint to take home as a souvenir, but Seymour himself – the main course – didn't actually put in a physical appearance anywhere. On the other hand, in the earlier, much shorter story I did, back in the late forties, he not only appeared in the flesh but walked, talked, went for a dip in the ocean, and fired a bullet through his brain in the last paragraph. However, several members of my immediate, if somewhat far-flung, family, who regularly pick over my published prose for small technical errors, have gently pointed out to me (much too damned gently, since they usually come down on me like grammarians) that the young man, the 'Seymour,' who did the walking and talking in that early story, not to mention the shooting, was not Seymour at all but, oddly, someone with a striking resemblance to – alley oop, I'm afraid – myself. Which is true, I think, or true enough to make me feel a craftsman's ping of reproof. And while there's no *good* excuse for that kind of *faux pas*, I can't forbear to mention that that particular story was written just a couple of months after Seymour's death, and not too very long after I myself, like both the 'Seymour' in the story and the Seymour in Real Life, had returned from the European Theater of Operations. I was using a very poorly rehabilitated, not to say unbalanced, German typewriter at the time.

Oh, this happiness is strong stuff. It's marvellously liberating. I'm *free*, I feel, to tell you exactly what you must be longing to hear now. That is, if, as I know you do, you love best in this world those little beings of pure spirit with a normal temperature of 125°, then it naturally follows that the creature you love next best is the person – the God-lover or God-hater (almost never, apparently, anything in between), the saint or profligate, moralist or complete immoralist – who can write a poem that *is* a poem. Among human beings, he's the curlew sandpiper, and I hasten to tell you what little I presume to know about his flights, his heat, his incredible heart.

Since early in 1948, I've been sitting – my family thinks literally – on a loose-leaf notebook inhabited by a hundred and eighty-four short poems that my brother wrote during the last three years of his life, both in and out of the Army, but mostly in, well in. I intend very soon now – it's just a matter of days or weeks, I tell myself – to stand aside from about a hundred and fifty of the poems and let the first willing publisher who owns a pressed morning suit and a fairly clean pair of gray gloves bear them away, right off to his shady presses, where they'll very likely be constrained in a two-tone dust jacket, complete with a back flap featuring a few curiously damning remarks of endorsement, as solicited and acquired from those 'name' poets and writers who have no compunction about commenting in public on their fellow-artists' works (customarily reserving their more deeply quarter-hearted commendations for their friends, suspected inferiors, foreigners, fly-by-night oddities, and toilers in another field), then on to the Sunday literary sections, where, if there's room, if the critique of the big, new, *definitive* biography of Grover Cleveland doesn't run too long, they'll be tersely introduced to the poetry-loving public by one of the little band of regulars, moderate-salaried pedants, and income-supplementers who can be trusted to review new books of poetry not necessarily either wisely or passionately but tersely. (I don't think I'll strike quite this sour note again. But if I do, I'll try to be equally transparent about it.) Now, considering that I've been sitting on the poems for over ten years, it might be well – refreshingly normal or unperverse, at least – if I gave what I think are the two main reasons I've elected to get up, rise, from them. And I'd prefer to pack both reasons into the same paragraph, duffelbag-style, partly because I'd like them to stick close to each other, partly because I have a perhaps impetuous notion that I won't be needing them again on the voyage.

First, there is the matter of family pressure. It's doubtless a very common thing, if not much more common than I'd care to hear about, but I have four living, lettered, rather incontinently articulate younger brothers and sisters, of part-Jewish, part-Irish, and conceivably part-Minotaur extraction – two boys, one, Waker, an ex-roving Carthusian monk-reporter, now impounded, and the other, Zooey, a no less vigorously called and chosen nonsectarian actor, aged, respectively, thirty-six and twenty-nine; and two girls, one a budding young actress, Franny, and the other, Boo Boo, a bouncy, solvent Westchester matron, aged, respectively, twenty-five and thirty-eight. Off and on since 1949, from seminary and boarding school, from the obstetrical floor of Woman's Hospital and the exchange-students' writing room below the waterline on the *Queen Elizabeth*, between, as it were; exams and dress rehearsals and matins and two-o'clock feedings, all four of these dignitaries have been laying down, through the mail, a series of unspecified but discernibly black ultimatums of what will happen to me unless I *do* something, *soon*, about Seymour's Poems. It should be noted, perhaps immediately, that besides being a writing man, I'm a part-time English Department member at a girls' college in upper New York, not far from the Canadian border. I live alone (but catless, I'd like everybody to know) in a totally modest, not to say cringing, little house, set deep in the woods and on the more inaccessible side of a mountain. Not counting students, faculty, and middle-aged waitresses, I see very few people during the working week, or year. I belong, in short, to a species of literary shut-in that, I don't doubt, can be coerced or bullied pretty successfully by mail. Everybody, anyhow, has a saturation point, and I can no longer open my post-office box without excessive trepidation at the prospect of finding, nestled among the farm-equipment circulars and the bank statements, a long, chatty, threatening postcard from one of my brothers or sisters, two of whom, it seems peculiarly worth adding, use ball-point pens. My second main reason for deciding to let go of the poems, get them published, is, in a way, much less emotional, really, than physical. (And it leads, I'm proud as a peacock to say, straight to the swamps of rhetoric.) The effects of radioactive particles on the human body, so topical in 1959, are nothing new to old poetry-lovers. Used with moderation, a first-class verse is an excellent and usually fast-working form of heat therapy. Once, in the Army, when I had what might be termed ambulatory pleurisy for something over three months, my first real relief came only when I had placed a perfectly innocent-looking Blake lyric in my shirt pocket and worn it like a poultice for a day or so. Extremes, though, are always risky and ordinarily downright baneful, and the dangers of prolonged contact with any poetry that seems to exceed what we most familiarly know of the first-class are formidable. In any case, I'd be relieved to see my brother's poems moved out of this general small area, at least for a while. I feel mildly but extensively burned. And on what seems to me the soundest basis: During much of his adolescence, and all his adult life, Seymour was drawn, first, to Chinese poetry, and then, as deeply, to

Japanese poetry, and to both in ways that he was drawn to no other poetry in the world.* I have no quick way of knowing, of course, how familiar or unfamiliar my dear, if victimized, general reader is with Chinese or Japanese poetry. Considering, however, that even a *short* discussion of it may possibly shed a good deal of light on my brother's nature, I don't think this is the time for me to go all reticent and forbearing. At their most effective, I believe, Chinese and Japanese classical verses are intelligible utterances that please or enlighten or enlarge the invited eavesdropper to within an inch of his life. They may be, and often are, fine for the ear particularly, but for the most part I'd say that unless a Chinese or Japanese poet's real forte is knowing a good persimmon or a good crab or a good mosquito bite on a good arm when he sees one, then no matter how long or unusual or fascinating his semantic or intellectual intestines may be, or how beguiling they sound when twanged, no one in the Mysterious East speaks seriously of him as a poet, if at all. My inner, incessant elation, which I think I've rightly, if repeatedly, called happiness, is threatening, I'm aware, to turn this whole composition into a fool's soliloquy. I think, though, that even I haven't the gall to try

* Since this is a record, of sorts, I ought to mumble, down here, that he read Chinese and Japanese poetry, for the most part, as it was written. Another time around, probably at irksome length – to me so, anyway – I'm going to have to dwell on an odd inborn characteristic common, to some extent, to all the original seven children in our family, and as pronounced as a limp in three of us, which made it possible for us to learn foreign languages with extreme ease. But this footnote is mainly for young readers. If, in the line of duty, I should incidentally titillate a few young people's interest in Chinese and Japanese poetry, it would be very good news to me. At all events, let the young person please know, if he doesn't already, that a goodish amount of first-class Chinese poetry has been translated into English, with much fidelity and spirit, by several distinguished people; Witter Bynner and Lionel Giles come most readily to mind. The best short Japanese poems – particularly haiku, but senryu, too – can be read with special satisfaction when R. H. Blyth has been at them. Blyth is sometimes perilous, naturally, since he's a highhanded old poem himself, but he's also sublime – and who goes to poetry for safety anyway? (This last little piece of pedantry, I repeat, is for the young, who write to authors and never get any replies from the beasts. I'm also functioning, partly, on behalf of my title character, who was a teacher, too, poor bastard.)

to say what makes the Chinese or Japanese poet the marvel and the joy he is. Something, however (wouldn't you know?), does happen to come to mind. (I don't imagine it's precisely the thing I'm looking for, but I can't simply throw it out.) Once, a terrible number of years ago, when Seymour and I were eight and six, our parents gave a party for nearly sixty people in our three and a half rooms at the old Hotel Alamac, in New York. They were officially retiring from vaudeville, and it was an affecting as well as a celebrative occasion. We two were allowed to get out of bed around eleven or so, and come in and have a look. We had more than a look. By request, and with no objections whatever on our part, we danced, we sang, first singly, then together, as children of our station often do. But mostly we just stayed up and watched. Toward two in the morning, when the leavetakings began, Seymour begged Bessie – our mother – to let him bring the leavers their coats, which were hung, draped, tossed, piled all over the small apartment, even on the foot of our sleeping younger sister's bed. He and I knew about a dozen of the guests intimately, ten or so more by sight or reputation, and the rest not at all or hardly. We had been in bed, I should add, when everyone arrived. But from watching the guests for some three hours, from grinning at them, from, I think, loving them, Seymour – without asking any questions first – brought very nearly all the guests, one or two at a time, and without any mistakes, their own true coats, and all the men involved their hats. (The women's hats he had some trouble with.) Now, I don't necessarily suggest that this kind of feat is typical of the Chinese or Japanese poet, and certainly I don't mean to imply that it makes him what he is. But I do think that if a Chinese or Japanese verse composer doesn't know whose coat is whose, on sight, his poetry stands a remarkably slim chance of ever ripening. And eight, I'd guess, is very nearly the outside age limit for mastering this small feat.

(No, no, I can't stop now. It seems to me, in my Condition, that I'm no longer merely asserting my brother's position as a poet; I feel I'm removing, at least for a minute or two, all the detonators from all the bombs in this bloody world – a very tiny, purely temporary public courtesy, no doubt, but mine own.) It's generally agreed that Chinese and Japanese poets like simple subjects best, and I'd feel more oafish than usual if I tried to refute that, but 'simple' happens to be a word I personally hate like poison, since – where I come from, anyway – it's customarily applied to the unconscionably brief, the timesaving in general, the trivial, the bald, and the abridged. My personal phobias aside, I don't really believe there *is* a word, in any language – thank God – to describe the Chinese or Japanese poet's choice of material. I wonder who can find a word for this kind of thing: A proud, pompous Cabinet member, walking in his courtyard and reliving a particularly devastating speech he made that morning in the Emperor's presence, steps, *with regret*, on a pen-and-ink sketch someone has lost or discarded. (Woe is me, there's a prose writer in our midst; I have to use italics where the Oriental poet wouldn't.) The great Issa will joyfully advise us that there's a fat-faced peony in the garden. (No more, no less. Whether we go to see his fat-faced peony for ourselves is another matter; unlike certain prose writers and Western poetasters, whom I'm in no position to name off, he doesn't police us.) The very mention of Issa's name convinces me that the true poet has no choice of material. The material plainly chooses him, not he it. A fat-faced peony will not show itself to anyone but Issa – not to Buson, not to Shiki, not even to Bashō. With certain prosaic modifications, the same rule holds for the proud and pompous Cabinet member. He will not dare to step with divinely human regret on a piece of sketch paper till the great commoner, bastard, and poet Lao Ti-kao has arrived on the scene to watch. The miracle of Chinese and Japanese verse is that one pure poet's voice is absolutely the same as another's and at once absolutely distinctive and different. Tang-li divulges, when he is ninety-three and is praised to his face for his wisdom and charity, that his piles are killing him. For another, a last, example, Ko-huang observes, with tears coursing down his face, that his late master had extremely bad table manners. (There is a risk, always, of being a trifle too beastly to the West. A line exists in Kafka's Diaries – one of many of his, really – that could easily usher in the Chinese New Year: 'The young girl who only because she was walking arm in arm with her sweetheart looked quietly around.') As for my brother Seymour – ah, well, my brother Seymour. For this Semitic-Celtic Oriental I need a spanking-new paragraph.

Unofficially, Seymour wrote and talked Chinese and Japanese poetry all the thirty-one years he stopped with us, but I'd say that he made a formal beginning at composing it one morning when he was eleven, in the first-floor reading room of a public library on upper Broadway, near our house. It was a Saturday, no school, nothing more pressing ahead of us than lunch, and we were having a fine time idly swimming around or treading water between the stacks, occasionally doing a little serious fishing for new authors, when he suddenly signalled to me to come over and see what he had. He'd caught himself a whole mess of translated verses by P'ang, the wonder of the eleventh century. But fishing, as we know, in libraries or anywhere else, is a tricky business, with never a certainty of who's going to catch whom. (The hazards of fishing in general were themselves a favorite subject of Seymour's. Our younger brother Walt was a great bent-pin fisherman as a small boy, and for his ninth or tenth birthday he received a poem from Seymour – one of the major delights of his life, I believe – about a little rich boy who catches a lafayette in the Hudson River, experiences a fierce pain in his own lower lip on reeling him in, then dismisses the matter from his mind, only to discover when he is home and the still-alive fish has been given the run of the bathtub that he, the fish, is wearing a blue serge cap with the same school insignia over the peak as the boy's own; the boy finds his own name-tape sewn inside the tiny wet cap.) Permanently, from that morning on, Seymour was hooked. By the time he was fourteen, one or two of us in the family were fairly regularly going through his jackets and windbreakers for anything good he might have jotted down during a slow gym period or a long wait at the dentist's. (A day has passed since this last sentence, and in the interim I've put through a long-distance call from my Place of Business to my sister Boo Boo, in Tuckahoe, to ask her if there's any poem from Seymour's very early boyhood that she'd especially like to go into this account. She said she'd call me back. Her choice turned out to be not nearly so apposite to my present purposes as I'd like, and therefore a trifle irritating, but I think I'll get over it. The one she picked, I happen to know, was written when the poet was eight: 'John Keats/ John Keats/ John/ Please put your scarf on.') When he was twenty-two, he had one special, not thin, sheaf of poems that looked very, very good to me, and I, who have never written a line longhand in my life without instantly visualizing it in eleven-point type, rather fractiously urged him to submit them for publication somewhere. No, he didn't think he could do that. Not yet; maybe never. They were too un-Western, too lotusy. He said he felt that they were faintly affronting. He hadn't quite made up his mind where the affronting came in, but he felt at times that the poems read as though they'd been written by an ingrate, of sorts, someone who was turning his back – in effect, at least – on his own environment and the people in it who were close to him. He said he ate his food out of our big refrigerators, drove our eight-cylinder American cars, unhesitatingly used our medicines when he was sick, and relied on the U.S. Army to protect his parents and sisters from Hitler's Germany, and nothing, not one single thing in all his poems, reflected these realities. Something was terribly wrong. He said that so often after he'd finished a poem he thought of Miss Overman. It should be said that Miss Overman had been the librarian in the first public-library branch in New York we regularly used when we were children. He said he felt he owed Miss Overman a painstaking, sustained search for a form of poetry that was in accord with his own peculiar standards and yet not wholly incompatible, even at first sight, with Miss Overman's tastes. When he got through saying that, I pointed out to him calmly, patiently – that is, of course, at the bloody top of my voice – what I thought were Miss Overman's shortcomings as a judge, or even a reader, of poetry. He then reminded me that on his first day in the public library (alone, aged six) Miss Overman, wanting or not as a judge of poetry, had opened a book to a plate of Leonardo's catapult and placed it brightly before him, and that it was no joy to him to finish writing a poem and know that Miss Overman would have trouble turning to it with pleasure or involvement, coming, as she probably would come, fresh from her beloved Mr Browning or her equally dear, and no less explicit, Mr Wordsworth. The argument – my argument, his discussion – ended there. You can't argue with someone who believes, or just passionately suspects, that the poet's function is not to write what he must write but, rather, to write what he would write if his life depended on his taking responsibility for writing what he must in a style designed to shut out as few of his old librarians as humanly possible.

For the faithful, the patient, the hermetically pure, all the important things in this world – not life and death, perhaps, which are merely words, but the important things – work out rather beautifully. Before his finish, Seymour had over three years of what must have been the profoundest satisfaction that a veteran craftsman is permitted to feel. He found for himself a form of versification that was right for him, that met his most long-standing demands of poetry in general, and that, I believe, had she still been alive, Miss Overman herself would very likely have thought striking, perhaps even comely, to look upon, and certainly 'involving,' provided she gave her attention to it as unfrugally as she gave it to her old swains, Browning and Wordsworth. What he found for himself, worked out for himself, is very difficult to describe.* It may help, to start with, to say that Seymour probably loved the classical Japanese three-line, seventeen-syllable haiku as he loved no other form of poetry, and that he himself wrote – bled – haiku (almost always in English, but sometimes, I hope I'm duly reluctant to bring in, in Japanese, German, or Italian). It could be said, and most likely will be, that a late-period poem of Seymour's looks substantially like an English translation of a sort of double haiku, if such a thing existed, and I don't think I'd quibble over that, but I tend to sicken at the strong probability that some tired but indefatigably waggish English Department

* The normal and only rational thing to do at this point would be to plank down one, two, or all hundred and eighty-four of the poems for the reader to see for himself. I can't do it. I'm permitted to sit on the poems, edit them, look after them, and eventually pick out a hard-cover publisher for them, but, on extremely personal grounds, I've been forbidden by the poet's widow, who legally owns them, to quote any portion of them here.

member in 1970 – not impossibly myself, God help me – will get off a good one about a poem of Seymour's being to the haiku what a double Martini is to the usual Martini. And the fact that it isn't true won't necessarily stop a pedant, if he feels that the class is properly warmed up and ready. Anyway, while I'm able, I'm going to say this rather slowly and carefully: A late poem of Seymour's is a six-line verse, of no certain accent but usually more iambic than not, that, partly out of affection for dead Japanese masters and partly from his own natural bent, as a poet, for working inside attractive restricted areas, he has deliberately held down to thirty-four syllables, or twice the number of the classical haiku. Apart from that, nothing in any of the hundred and eighty-four poems currently under my roof is much like anything except Seymour himself. To say the least, the acoustics, even, are as singular as Seymour. That is, each of the poems is as unsonorous, as quiet, as he believed a poem should be, but there are intermittent short blasts of euphony (for want of a less atrocious word for it), which have the effect on me personally of someone – surely no one completely sober – opening my door, blowing three or four or five unquestionably sweet and expert notes on a cornet into the room, then disappearing. (I've never known a poet to give the impression of playing a cornet in the middle of a poem before, let alone playing one beautifully, and I'd just as soon say next to nothing about it. In fact, nothing.) Within this six-line structure and these very odd harmonics, Seymour does with a poem, I think, exactly what he was meant to do with one. By far the majority of the hundred and eighty-four poems are immeasurably not light- but high-hearted, and can be read by anyone, anywhere, even aloud in rather progressive orphanages on stormy nights, but I wouldn't unreservedly recommend the last thirty or thirty-five poems to any living soul who hasn't died at least twice in his lifetime, preferably slowly. My own favorites, if I have any, and I most assuredly do, are the two final poems in the collection. I don't think I'll be stepping on anybody's toes if I very simply say what they are about. The next-to-last poem is about a young married woman and mother who is plainly having what it refers to here in my old marriage manual as an extra-marital love affair.

Seymour doesn't describe her, but she comes into the poem just when that cornet of his is doing something extraordinarily effective, and I see her as a terribly pretty girl, moderately intelligent, immoderately unhappy, and not unlikely living a block or two away from the Metropolitan Museum of Art. She comes home very late one night from a tryst – in my mind, bleary and lipstick-smeared – to find a balloon on her bedspread. Someone has simply left it there. The poet doesn't say, but it can't be anything but a large, inflated toy balloon, probably green, like Central Park in spring. The other poem, the last one in the collection, is about a young suburban widower who sits down on his patch of lawn one night, implicitly in his pajamas and robe, to look at the full moon. A bored white cat, clearly a member of his household and almost surely a former kingpin of his household, comes up to him and rolls over, and he lets her bite his left hand as he looks at the moon. This final poem, in fact, could well be of extra interest to my general reader on two quite special counts. I'd like very much to discuss them.

As suits most poetry, and emphatically befits any poetry with a marked Chinese or Japanese 'influence,' Seymour's verses are all as bare as possible, and invariably ungarnished. However, on a weekend visit up here, some six months ago, my younger sister, Franny, while accidentally rifling my desk drawers, came across this widower poem I've just finished (criminally) plotting out; it had been detached from the main body of the collection for retyping. For reasons not strictly pertinent at the moment, she had never seen the poem before, and so, naturally, she read it on the spot. Later, in talking to me about the poem, she said she wondered why Seymour had said it was the left hand that the young widower let the white cat bite. That bothered her. She said it sounded more like me than like Seymour, that 'left' business. Apart, of course, from the slanderous reflection on my ever-increasing professional passion for detail, I think she meant that the adjective struck her as obtrusive, overexplicit, unpoetic. I argued her down, and I'm prepared, frankly, to argue *you* down, too, if necessary. I'm certain in my own mind that Seymour thought it vital to suggest that it was the left, the second-best, hand the young widower let the white cat press her needle-sharp teeth into, thereby leaving the right hand free for breast- or forehead-smiting – an analysis that may seem to many readers very, very tiresome indeed. And maybe so. But I know how my brother felt about human hands. Besides, there is another, exceedingly considerable aspect of the matter. It may seem a little tasteless to go into it at any length – rather like insisting on reading the entire script of 'Abie's Irish Rose' to a perfect stranger over the phone – but Seymour was a half Jew, and while I can't speak up with the great Kafka's absolute authority on this theme, it's my very sober guess, at forty, that any thinking man with a muchness of Semitic blood in his veins either lives or has lived on oddly intimate, almost mutually knowledgeable terms with his hands, and though he may go along for years and years figuratively *or* literally keeping them in his pockets (not always, I'm afraid, altogether unlike two pushy old friends or relatives he'd prefer not to bring to the party), he will, I think, use them, break them out very readily, in a crisis, often do something drastic with them in a crisis, such as mentioning, unpoetically, in the middle of a poem that it was the left hand the cat bit – and poetry, surely, is a crisis, perhaps the only actionable one we can call our own. (I apologize for that verbiage. Unfortunately, there's probably more.) My second reason for thinking that the particular poem may be of extra – and, I hope, real – interest to my general reader is the queer personal force that has gone into it. I've never seen anything quite like it in print, and, I might injudiciously mention, from early childhood till I was well past thirty I seldom read fewer than two hundred thousand words a day, and often closer to four. At forty, admittedly, I rarely feel even peckish, and when I'm not required to inspect English compositions belonging either to young ladies or to myself, I customarily read very little except harsh postcards from relatives, seed catalogues, bird-watchers' bulletins (of one sort or another), and poignant Get-Well-Soon notes from old readers of mine who have somewhere picked up the bogus information that I spend six months of the year in a Buddhist monastery and the other six in a mental institution. The pride of a nonreader, however, I'm well aware – or, for that matter, the pride of a markedly curtailed consumer of books – is even more offensive than the pride of certain voluminous readers, and so I've tried (I think I mean this seriously) to keep up a few of my oldest literary conceits. One of the grossest of these is that I can usually tell whether a poet or prose writer is drawing from the first-, second-, or tenth-hand experience or is foisting off on us what he'd like to think is pure invention. Yet when I first read that young-widower-and-white-cat verse, back in 1948 – or, rather, sat listening to it – I found it very hard to believe that Seymour hadn't buried at least one wife that nobody in our family knew about. He hadn't, of course. Not (and first blushes here, if any, will be the reader's, not mine) – not in this incarnation, at any rate. Nor, to my quite extensive and somewhat serpentine knowledge of the man, had he any intimate acquaintance with young widowers. For a final and entirely ill-advised comment on the matter, he himself was about as far from being a widower as a young American male can be. And while it's possible that, at odd moments, tormenting or exhilarating, every married man – Seymour, just conceivably, though almost entirely for the sake of argument, not excluded – reflects on how life would be with the little woman out of the picture (the implication here being that a first-class poet might work up a fine elegy from that sort of woolgathering), the possibility seems to me mere grist to psychologists' mills, and certainly much beside my point. My point being – and I'll try, against the usual odds, not to labor it – that the more personal Seymour's poems appear to be, or *are*, the less revealing the content is of any known details of his actual daily life in this Western world. My brother Waker, in fact, contends (and let us hope that his abbot never gets wind of it) that Seymour, in many of his most effective poems, seems to be drawing on the ups and downs of former, singularly memorable existences in exurban Benares, feudal Japan, and metropolitan Atlantis. I pause, of course, to give the reader a chance to throw up his hands, or, more likely, to wash them of the whole lot of us. Just the same, I imagine all the living children in our family would rather volubly agree with Waker about that, though one or two, perhaps, with slight reservations. For instance, on the afternoon of his suicide

Seymour wrote a straight, classical-style haiku on the desk blotter in his hotel room. I don't much like my literal translation of it – he wrote it in Japanese – but in it he briefly tells of a little girl on an airplane who has a doll in the seat with her and turns its head around to look at the poet. A week or so before the poem was actually written, Seymour had actually been a passenger on a commercial airplane, and my sister Boo Boo has somewhat treacherously suggested that there may have *been* a little girl with a doll aboard his plane. I myself doubt it. Not necessarily flatly, but I doubt it. And if such *was* the case – which I don't believe for a minute – I'd make a bet the child never thought to draw her friend's attention to Seymour.

Do I go on about my brother's poetry too much? Am I being garrulous? Yes. Yes. I go on about my brother's poetry too much. I'm being garrulous. And I care. But my reasons against leaving off multiply like rabbits as I go along. Furthermore, though I am, as I've already conspicuously posted, a happy writer, I'll take my oath I'm not now and never have been a merry one; I've mercifully been allowed the usual professional quota of unmerry thoughts. For example, it hasn't just this moment struck me that once I get around to recounting what I know of Seymour himself, I can't expect to leave myself either the space or the required pulse rate or, in a broad but true sense, the inclination to mention his poetry again. At this very instant, alarmingly, while I clutch my own wrist and lecture myself on garrulousness, I may be losing the chance of a lifetime – my last chance, I think, really – to make one final, hoarse, objectionable, sweeping public pronouncement on my brother's rank as an American poet. I mustn't let it slip. Here it is: When I look back, listen back, over the half-dozen or slightly more original poets we've had in America, as well as the numerous talented eccentric poets and – in modern times, especially – the many gifted style deviates, I feel something close to a conviction that we have had only three or four *very* nearly non-expendable poets, and I think Seymour will eventually stand with those few. Not overnight, *verständlich* – *zut*, what would you? It's my guess, my perhaps flagrantly over-considered guess, that the first few waves of reviewers will obliquely condemn his verses by calling them Interesting or Very Interesting, with a tacit or just plain badly articulated declaration, still more damning, that they are rather small, sub-acoustical things that have failed to arrive on the contemporary Western scene with their own built-in transatlantic podium, complete with lectern, drinking glass, and pitcher of iced sea water. Yet a real artist, I've noticed, will survive anything. (Even praise, I happily suspect.) And I'm reminded, too, that once, when we were boys, Seymour waked me from a sound sleep, much excited, yellow pajamas flashing in the dark. He had what my brother Walt used to call his Eureka Look, and he wanted to tell me that he thought he finally knew why Christ said to call no man Fool. (It was a problem that had been baffling him all week, because it sounded to him like a piece of advice, I believe, more typical of Emily Post than of someone busily about his Father's Business.) Christ had said it, Seymour thought I'd want to know, because there are no fools. Dopes, yes – fools, no. It seemed to him well worth waking me up for, but if I admit that it was (and I do, without reservations), I'll have to concede that if you give even poetry critics enough time, they'll prove themselves unfoolish. To be truthful, it's a thought that comes hard to me, and I'm grateful to be able to push on to something else. I've reached, at long last, the real head of this compulsive and, I'm afraid, occasionally somewhat pustulous disquisition on my brother's poetry. I've seen it coming from the very beginning. I would to God the reader had something terrible to tell me first. (Oh, you out there – with your enviable golden silence.)

I have a recurrent, and, in 1959, almost chronic, premonition that when Seymour's poems have been widely and rather officially acknowledged as First Class (stacked up in college bookstores, assigned in Contemporary Poetry courses), matriculating young men and women will strike out, in singlets and twosomes, notebooks at the ready, for my somewhat creaking front door. (It's regrettable that this matter has to come up at all, but it's surely too late to pretend to an ingenuousness, to say nothing of a grace, I don't have, and I must reveal that my reputedly heart-shaped prose has knighted me one of the best-loved sciolists in print since Ferris L. Monahan, and a good many young English Department people already know where I live, hole up; I have their tire tracks in my rose beds to prove it.) By and large, I'd say without a shred of hesitation, there are three kinds of students who have both the desire and the temerity to look as squarely as possible into any sort of literary horse's mouth. The first kind is the young man or woman who loves and respects to distraction any fairly responsible sort of literature and who, if he or she can't see Shelley plain, will make do with seeking out manufacturers of inferior but estimable products. I know these boys and girls well, or think I do. They're naïve, they're alive, they're enthusiastic, they're usually less than right, and they're the hope always, I think, of blasé or vested-interested literary society the world over. (By some good fortune I can't believe I've deserved, I've had one of these ebullient, cock-sure, irritating, instructive, often charming girls or boys in every second or third class I've taught in the past twelve years.) The second kind of young person who actually rings doorbells in the pursuit of literary data suffers, somewhat proudly, from a case of academicitis, contracted from any one of half a dozen Modern English professors or graduate instructors to whom he's been exposed since his freshman year. Not seldom, if he himself is already teaching or is about to start teaching, the disease is so far along that one doubts whether it could be arrested, even if someone were fully equipped to try. Only last year, for example, a young man stopped by to see me about a piece I'd written, several years back, that had a good deal to do with Sherwood Anderson. He came at a time when I was cutting part of my winter's supply of firewood with a gasoline-operated chain saw – an instrument that after eight years of repeated use I'm still terrified of. It was the height of the spring thaw, a beautiful sunny day, and I was feeling, frankly, just a trifle Thoreauish (a real treat for me, because after thirteen years of country living I'm still a man who gauges bucolic distances by New York City blocks). In short, it looked like a promising, if literary, afternoon, and I recall that I had high hopes of getting the young man, à la Tom Sawyer and his bucket of whitewash, to have a go at my chain saw. He appeared healthy, not to say strapping. His deceiving looks, however, very nearly cost me my left foot, for between spurts and buzzes of my saw, just as I finished delivering a short and to me rather enjoyable eulogy on Sherwood Anderson's gentle and effective style, the young man asked me – after a thoughtful, a cruelly promising pause – if I thought there was an endemic American *Zeitgeist*. (Poor young man. Even if he takes exceptionally good care of himself, he can't at the outside have more than fifty years of successful campus activity ahead of him.) The third kind of person who will be a fairly constant visitor around here, I believe, once Seymour's poems have been quite thoroughly unpacked and tagged, requires a paragraph to himself or herself.

It would be absurd to say that most young people's attraction to poetry is far exceeded by their attraction to those few or many details of a poet's life that may be defined here, loosely, operationally, as lurid. It's the sort of absurd notion, though, that I wouldn't mind taking out for a good academic run someday. I surely think, at any rate, that if I were to ask the sixty odd girls (or, that is, the sixty-odd girls) in my two Writing for Publication courses – most of them seniors, all of them English majors – to quote a line, any line from 'Ozymandias,' or even just to tell me roughly what the poem is about, it is doubtful whether ten of them could do either, but I'd bet my unrisen tulips that some fifty of them could tell me that Shelley was all for free love, and had one wife who wrote 'Frankenstein' and another who drowned

* Just for the sake of making a point I could be embarrassing my students unnecessarily here. Schoolteachers have done it before. Or maybe I've just picked out the wrong poem. If it's true, as I've wickedly posed, that 'Ozymandias' has left my students vividly unimpressed, perhaps a good deal of the blame for this can be laid to 'Ozymandias' itself. Perhaps Mad Shelley wasn't quite mad enough. Assuredly, in any case, his madness wasn't a madness of the heart. My girls undoubtedly know that Robert Burns drank and romped to excess, and are probably delighted about it, but I'm equally sure they also know all about the magnificent mouse his plow turned up. (Is it just possible, I wonder, that those 'two vast and trunkless legs of stone' standing in the desert are Percy's own? Is it conceivable that his life is outliving much of his best poetry? And if so, is it because – Well, I'll desist. But young poets beware. If you want us to remember your best poems at least as fondly as we do your Racy, Colorful Lives, it might be as well to give us one good field mouse, flushed by the heart, in every stanza.)

herself.* I'm neither shocked nor outraged at the idea, please mind. I don't think I'm even complaining. For if nobody's a fool, then neither am I, and I'm entitled to a non-fool's Sunday awareness that, whoever we are, no matter how like a blast furnace the heat from the candles on our latest birthday cake, and however presumably lofty the intellectual, moral, and spiritual heights we've all reached, our gusto for the lurid or the partly lurid (which, of course, includes both low and superior gossip) is probably the last of our fleshy appetites to be sated or effectively curbed. (But, my God, why do I rant on? Why am I not going straight to the poet for an illustration? One of Seymour's hundred and eighty-four poems – a shocker on the first impact only; on the second, as heartening a paean to the living as I've read – is about a distinguished old ascetic on his deathbed, surrounded by chanting priests and disciples, who lies straining to hear what the washerwoman in the courtyard is saying about his neighbor's laundry. The old gentleman, Seymour makes it clear, is faintly wishing the priests would keep their voices down a bit.) I can see, though, that I'm having a *little* of the usual trouble entailed in trying to make a very convenient generalization stay still and docile long enough to support a wild specific premise. I don't relish being sensible about it, but I suppose I must. It seems to me indisputably true that a good many people, the wide world over, of varying ages, cultures, natural endowments, respond with a special impetus, a zing, even, in some cases, to artists and poets who as well as having a reputation for producing great or fine art have something garishly Wrong with them as persons: a spectacular flaw in character or citizenship, a construably romantic affliction or addiction – extreme self-centeredness, marital infidelity, stone-deafness, stone-blindness, a terrible thirst, a mortally bad cough, a soft spot for prostitutes, a partiality for grand-scale adultery or incest, a certified or uncertified weakness for opium or sodomy, and so on, God have mercy on the lonely bastards. If suicide isn't at the top of the list of compelling infirmities for creative men, the suicide poet or artist, one can't help noticing, has always been given a very considerable amount of avid attention, not seldom on sentimental grounds almost exclusively, as if he were (to put it much more horribly than I really want to) the floppy-eared runt of the litter. It's a thought, anyway, *finally said*, that I've lost sleep over many times, and possibly will again.

(How can I record what I've just recorded and still be happy? But I am. Unjolly, unmerry, to the marrow, but my afflatus seems to be punctureproof. Recollective of only one other person I've known in my life.) You can't imagine what big, hand-rubbing plans I had for this immediate space. They appear to have been designed, though, to look exquisite on the bottom of my wastebasket. I'd *intended* right here to relieve those last two midnight paragraphs with a couple of sunshiny witticisms, a matched pair of the sort of thigh-slappers that so often, I imagine, turn my fellow-raconteurs green with envy or nausea. It was my intention, right here, to tell the reader that when, or if, young people should stop by to see me about Seymour's life or death, a curious personal affliction of my own, alas, would make such an audience utterly unfeasible. I planned to mention – just in passing, because this will be developed at, I hope, interminable length someday – that Seymour and I, as children, together spent close to seven years answering questions on a network-radio quiz program, and that ever since we formally went off the air, I've felt pretty much about people who as little as ask me the time of day almost precisely the way Betsey Trotwood felt about donkeys. Next, I intended to divulge that after some twelve years as a college instructor I'm now, in 1959, subject to frequent attacks of what my faculty colleagues have been flattering enough to think of, I believe, as Glass's disease – in lay language, a pathological spasm of the lumbar and lower ventral regions that causes an off-duty classroom lecturer to double up and hurriedly cross streets or crawl under large pieces of furniture when he sees anyone under forty approaching. Neither of the two sallies will work for me here, though. There's a certain amount of perverse truth to both, but not nearly enough. For the terrible and undiscountable fact has just reached me, between paragraphs, that I *yearn* to talk, to be queried, to be interrogated, about this particular dead man. It's just got through to me, that apart from my many other – and, I hope to God, less ignoble – motives, I'm stuck with the usual survivor's conceit that he's the only soul alive who knew the deceased intimately. *O let them come* – the callow and the enthusiastic, the academic, the curious, the long and the short and the all-knowing! Let them arrive in busloads, let them parachute in, wearing Leicas. The mind swarms with gracious welcoming speeches. One hand already reaches for the box of detergent and the other for the dirty tea service. The bloodshot eye practices clearing. *The old red carpet is out.*

A very delicate matter now. A trifle *coarse*, to be sure, but delicate, very delicate.

Considering that this matter may not come up in any desirable, or massive, detail later on, I think the reader should know right now, and preferably bear in mind to the very end, that all the children in our family were, are, descended from an astonishingly long and motley double-file of professional entertainers. For the most part, genetically speaking, or muttering, we sing, dance, and (can you doubt it?) tell Funny Jokes. But I think it peculiarly important to keep in mind – and so did Seymour, even as a child – that there is also among us a wide miscellany of performing circus people and performing, so to say, circus-fringe people. One of my great-grandfathers (*and* Seymour's), for an admittedly juicy example, was a quite famous Polish-Jewish carnival clown named Zozo, who had a penchant – up to the very end, one necessarily gathers – for diving from immense heights into small containers of water. Another of Seymour's and my great-grandfathers, an Irishman named MacMahon (whom my mother, to her everlasting credit, has never been tempted to refer to as a 'darlin' man'), was a self-employed type who used to set out a couple of octaves of empty whiskey bottles in a meadow and then, when a paying crowd had closed in, dance, we're told, rather musically on the sides of the bottles. (So, surely you'll take my word, we have, among other things, a few nuts on the family tree.) Our parents themselves, Les and Bessie Glass, had a fairly conventional but (*we* believe) remarkably good song-and-dance-and-patter act in vaudeville and music halls, reaching perhaps most nearly top billing in Australia (where Seymour and I spent about two years, in total bookings, of our very early childhood) but later, too, achieving much more than just passing notability on the old Pantages and Orpheum circuits, here in America. In the opinion of not a few people, they might have gone on as a vaudeville team for quite a bit longer than they did. Bessie had ideas of her own, though. Not only has she always had something of an aptitude for reading handwriting on walls – two-a-day vaudeville already in 1925 was almost finished, and Bessie had, both as a mother and as a dancer, the very strongest convictions against doing four-a-day shows for the big, new, ever-multiplying movie-*cum*-vaudeville palaces – but, more important than that, ever since she was a child in Dublin and her twin sister succumbed, backstage, of galloping undernutrition, Security, in any form, has had a fatal attraction for Bessie. At any rate, in the spring of 1925, at the end of a so-so run at the Albee, in Brooklyn, with five children bedded down with German measles in three and a half unstately rooms at the old Hotel Alamac, in Man*hat*tan, and a notion that she was pregnant again (mistaken, it turned out; the babies of the family, Zooey and Franny, were not born till 1930 and 1935, respectively), Bessie suddenly appealed to an honest-to-God 'influential' admirer, and my father took a job in what he invariably referred to, for years and years, with no real fear of being contradicted around the house, as the ministrative end of commercial radio, and Gallagher & Glass's extended tour was officially over. What I'm *mainly* trying to do here, though, is to find the firmest way of suggesting that this curious footlight-and-three-ring heritage has been an almost ubiquitous and entirely significant reality in the lives of all seven of the children in our family. The two youngest, as I've already mentioned, are, in fact, professional actors. But no *heavy* line can be drawn quite there. The elder of my two sisters, to most outward appearances, is a fully landed suburbanite, mother of three children, co-owner of a two-car, filled garage, but at all supremely joyful moments she will, all but literally, dance for her life; I've seen her, to my horror, break into a very passable soft-shoe routine (a sort of Ned Wayburn out of Pat and Marion Rooney) with a five-day-old niece of mine in her arms. My late younger brother Walt, who was killed in a postwar accident in

Japan (and of whom I plan to say as little as possible in this series of sittings, if I'm to get through them), was a dancer, too, in a perhaps less spontaneous but far more professional sense than my sister Boo Boo. His twin – our brother Waker, our monk, our impounded Carthusian – as a boy, privately canonized W. C. Fields and in that inspired and obstreperous but rather holy man's image used to practice juggling with cigar boxes, among a great many other things, by the hour, till he became spectacularly proficient at it. (Family rumor has it that he was originally cloistered off – that is, relieved of his duties as a secular priest in Astoria – to free him of a persistent temptation to administer the sacramental wafer to his parishioners' lips by standing back two or three feet and trajecting it in a lovely arc over his left shoulder.) As for myself – I'd prefer to take Seymour last – I'm quite sure it goes without saying that I dance a little bit, too. On request, of course. Apart from that, I might mention that I often feel I'm watched over, if somewhat erratically, by Great-Grandfather Zozo; I feel he mysteriously provides that I don't trip over my invisible baggy clown-pants when I stroll in the woods or walk into classrooms, and perhaps also sees to it that my putty nose occasionally points east when I sit down at the typewriter.

Nor, finally, did our Seymour himself live or die a whit less affected by his 'background' than any of the rest of us. I've already mentioned that although I believe his poems couldn't be more personal, or reveal him more completely, he goes through every one of them, even when the Muse of Absolute Joy is sitting on his back, without spilling a single really autobiographical bean. The which, I suggest, though possibly not to everyone's taste, is highly literate vaudeville – a traditional first act, a man balancing words, emotions, a golden cornet on his chin, instead of the usual evening cane, chromium table, and champagne glass filled with water. But I have something far more explicit and leading to tell you than that. I've been waiting for it: In Brisbane, in 1922, when Seymour and I were five and three, Les and Bessie played on the same bill for a couple of weeks with Joe Jackson – the redoubtable Joe Jackson of the nickel-plated trick bicycle that shone like something better than platinum to the very last row of the theater.

A good many years later, not long after the outbreak of the Second World War, when Seymour and I had just recently moved into a small New York apartment of our own, our father – Les, as he'll be called hereafter – dropped in on us one evening on his way home from a pinochle game. He quite apparently had held very bad cards all afternoon. He came in, at any rate, rigidly predisposed to keep his overcoat on. He sat. He scowled at the furnishings. He turned my hand over to check for cigarette-tar stains on my fingers, then asked Seymour how many cigarettes he smoked a day. He thought he found a fly in his highball. At length, when the conversation – in my view, at least – was going straight to hell, he got up abruptly and went over to look at a photograph of himself and Bessie that had been newly tacked up on the wall. He glowered at it for a full minute, or more, then turned around, with a brusqueness no one in the family would have found unusual, and asked Seymour if he remembered the time Joe Jackson had given him, Seymour, a ride on the handle bars of his bicycle, all over the stage, around and around. Seymour, sitting in an old corduroy armchair across the room, a cigarette going, wearing a blue shirt, gray slacks, moccasins with the counters broken down, a shaving cut on the side of his face that I could see, replied gravely and at once, and in the special way he always answered questions from Les – as if they were the questions, above all others, he preferred to be asked in his life. He said he wasn't sure he had ever got off Joe Jackson's beautiful bicycle. And aside from its enormous sentimental value to my father personally, this answer, in a great many ways, was true, true, true.

Between the last paragraph and this, just over two and a half months have gone by, Elapsed. A little bulletin that I grimace slightly to have to issue, since it reads back to me exactly as though I were about to intimate that I always use a chair when I work, drink upward of thirty cups of black coffee during Composing Hours, and make all my own furniture in my spare time; in short, it has the tone of a man of letters unreluctantly discussing his work habits, his hobbies, and his more printable human frailties with the interviewing officer from the Sunday Book

Section. I'm really not up to anything that *intime* just here. (I'm keeping especially close tabs on myself here, in fact. It seems to me that this composition has never been in more imminent danger than right now of taking on precisely the informality of underwear.) I've announced a major delay between paragraphs by way of informing the reader that I'm just freshly risen from nine weeks in bed with acute hepatitis. (You see what I mean about underwear. This last open remark of mine happens to be a straight line, almost *intacta*, right out of Minsky burlesque. Second Banana: 'I've been in bed for nine weeks with acute hepatitis.' Top Banana: 'Which one, you lucky dog? They're both cute, those Hepatitis girls.' If this be my promised clean bill of health, let me find a quick way back to the Valley of the Sick.) When I now confide, as I surely must, that I've been up and around for nearly a week, with the rose fully restored to cheek and jowl, will the reader, I wonder, misinterpret my confidence – mainly, I think, in two ways? One, will he think it's a mild rebuke to him for neglecting to flood my sickroom with camellias? (Everyone will be relieved to know, it's a safe guess, that I'm running out of Humor by the second.) Two, will he, the reader, choose to think, on the basis of this Sick Report, that my personal happiness – so carefully touted at the very beginning of this composition – perhaps wasn't happiness at all but just liverishness? This second possibility is of extremely grave concern to me. For certain, I was genuinely happy to be working on this Introduction. In my own supine way, I was miraculously happy all through my hepatitis (and the alliteration alone should have finished me off.) And I'm ecstatically happy at this moment, I'm happy to say. Which is not to deny (and I've come now, I'm afraid, to the real reason I've constructed this showcase for my poor old liver) – which is not to deny, I repeat, that my ailment left me with a single, terrible deficiency. I hate dramatic indentations with all my heart, but I suppose I do need a new paragraph for this matter.

The first night, just this last week, that I felt quite hale and bullish enough to go back to work on this Introduction, I found that I'd lost not my afflatus but my wherewithal to continue to write about Seymour. *He'd grown too much while I was away.* It was hardly credible. From the manageable giant he had been before I got sick, he had shot up, in nine short weeks, into the most familiar human being of my life, the one person who was always much, much too large to fit on ordinary typewriter paper – any typewriter paper of mine, anyway. To put it flatly, I panicked, and I panicked for five consecutive nights thereafter. I think, though, that I mustn't paint this any blacker than I have to. For there happens to be a very stunning silver lining. Let me tell you, without pausing, what I did tonight that makes me feel I'll be back at work tomorrow night bigger and cockier and more objectionable, possibly, than ever. About two hours ago, I simply read an old personal letter – more accurately, a very lengthy memo – that was left on my breakfast plate one morning in 1940. Under half a grapefruit, to be precise. In just another minute or two, I mean to have the unutterable ('pleasure' isn't the word I want) – the unutterable Blank of reproducing the long memo here verbatim. (O happy hepatitis! I've never known sickness – or sorrow, or disaster, for that matter – not to unfold, eventually, like a flower or a good memo. We're required only to keep looking. Seymour once said, on the air, when he was eleven, that the thing he loved best in the Bible was the word WATCH!) Before I get to the main item, though, it behooves me, from head to foot, to attend to a few incidental matters. This chance may never come again.

It seems a serious oversight, but I don't think I've said that it was my custom, my compulsion, whenever it was practical, and very often when it wasn't, to try out my new short stories on Seymour. That is, read them aloud to him. Which I did *molto agitato*, with a clearly indicated required Rest Period for everybody at the finish. This is by way of saying that Seymour always refrained from making any comments after my voice had come to a stop. Instead, he usually looked at the ceiling for five or ten minutes – he invariably stretched out flat on the floor for a Reading – then got up, (sometimes) gently stamped a foot that had gone to sleep, and left the room. Later – usually in a matter of hours, but on one or two occasions days – he would jot down a few notes on a piece of paper or a shirt cardboard and either leave it on my bed or at my place at the dinner table or (very rarely) send it to me through the U.S. Mail. Here are a few of his brief criticisms. (This is a warmup, frankly. I see no point in disclaiming it, though I probably should.)

Horrible, but right. An honest Medusa's Head.

I wish I knew. The woman is fine, but the painter seems haunted by your friend the man who painted Anna Karenina's portrait in Italy. Which is swell haunting, the best, but you have your own irascible painters.

I think it should be done over, Buddy. The Doctor is so good, but I think you like him too late. The whole first half, he's out in the cold, waiting for you to like him, and he's your main character. You see his nice dialogue with the nurse as a conversion. It should have been a religious story, but it's puritanical. I feel your censure on all his God-damns. That seems off to me. What is it but a low form of prayer when he or Les or anybody else God-damns everything? I can't believe God recognizes any form of blasphemy. It's a prissy word invented by the clergy.

I'm so sorry about this one. I wasn't listening right. I'm so sorry. The first sentence threw me way off. 'Henshaw woke up that morning with a splitting head.' I count so heavily on you to finish off all the fraudulent Henshaws in fiction. There just are no Henshaws. Will you read it to me again?

Please make your peace with your wit. It's not going to go away, Buddy. To dump it on your own advice would be as bad and unnatural as dumping your adjectives and adverbs because Prof. B. wants you to. What does he know about it? What do you really know about your own wit?

I've been sitting here tearing up notes to you. I keep starting to say things like 'This one is wonderfully constructed,' and 'The woman on the back of the truck is very funny,' and 'The conversation between the two cops is terrific.' So I'm hedging. I'm not sure why. I started to get a little nervous right after you began to read. It sounded like the beginning of something your arch-enemy Bob B. calls a rattling good story. Don't you think he would call this a step in the right direction? Doesn't that worry you? Even what is funny about the woman on the back of the truck doesn't sound like something *you* think is funny. It sounds much more like something that you think is universally considered very funny. I feel gypped. Does that make you mad? You can say our relatedness spoils my judgment. It worries me enough. But I'm also just a reader. Are you a writer or just a writer of rattling good stories. I mind getting a rattling good story from you. I want your *loot*.

I can't get this new one off my mind. I don't know what to say about it. I know what the dangers of getting into sentimentality must have been. You got through it fine. Maybe too fine. I wonder if I don't wish you'd slipped up a little. Can I write a little story for *you*? Once there was a great music critic, a distinguished authority on Wolfgang Amadeus Mozart. His little daughter went to P. S. 9, where she was in the Glee Club, and this great music-lover was very annoyed when she came home one day with another child to practice singing a medley of songs by Irving Berlin and Harold Arlen and Jerome Kern and people like that. Why shouldn't the children sing little simple Schubert Lieder instead of that 'trash'? So he went to the principal of the school and made a big stink about it. The principal was much impressed by such a distinguished person's arguments, and he agreed to turn the Music Appreciation Teacher, a very old lady, over his knee. The great music-lover left his office in very good spirits. On the way home, he thought over the brilliant arguments he had advanced in the principal's office and his elation grew and grew. His chest expanded. His step quickened. He began to whistle a little tune. The tune: 'K-K-K-Katy.'

The Memo now. As presented with pride and resignation. Pride because – Well, I'll pass that. Resignation because some of my faculty comrades may be listening – veteran interoffice cutups, all – and I have a notion that this particular enclosure is sooner or later bound to be entitled 'A Nineteen-Year-Old Prescription for Writers and Brothers and Hepatitis Convalescents Who Have Lost Their Way and Can't Go On.' (Ah, well. It takes a cutup to know one. Besides, I feel that my loins are oddly girded for this occasion.)

I think, first, that this was the lengthiest critical comment I ever had from Seymour about any Literary Effort of mine – and, for that matter, probably the longest non-oral communiqué I ever got from him during his life. (We very rarely wrote personal letters to each other, even during the war.) It was written in pencil, on several sheets of notepaper that our mother had relieved the

Bismarck Hotel, in Chicago, of, some years earlier. He was responding to what was surely the most ambitious *bloc* of writing I had done up to that time. The year was 1940, and we were both still living in our parents' rather thickly populated apartment in the East Seventies. I was twenty-one, as unattached as, shall I say, only a young, unpublished, green-complexioned writer can be. Seymour himself was twenty-three and had just begun his fifth year of teaching English at a university in New York. Herewith, then, in full. (I can foresee a few embarrassments for the discriminating reader, but the Worst, I think, will be over with the salutation. I figure that if the salutation doesn't embarrass *me* particularly, I don't see why it should embarrass any other living soul.)

DEAR OLD TYGER THAT SLEEPS:

I wonder if there are many readers who have ever turned the pages of a manuscript while the author snores in the same room. I wanted to see this one for myself. Your voice was almost too much this time. I think your prose is getting to be all the theatre your characters can withstand. I have so much I want to tell you, and nowhere to begin.

This afternoon I wrote what I thought was a whole letter to the head of the English Department, of all people, that sounded quite a lot like you. It gave me such pleasure I thought I ought to tell you. It was a beautiful letter. It felt like the Saturday afternoon last spring when I went to Die Zauberflöte with Carl and Amy and that very strange girl they brought for me and I wore your green intoxicator. I didn't tell you I wore it. [*He was referring here to one of four expensive neckties I'd bought the season before. I'd forbidden all my brothers – but especially Seymour, who had easiest access to them – to go anywhere near the drawer I kept them in. I stored them, only partly as a gag, in cellophane.*] I felt no guilt when I wore it, only a mortal fear that you'd suddenly walk on the stage and see me sitting there in the dark with your tie on. The letter was a little bit different. It occurred to me that if things were switched around and you were writing a letter that sounded like me, you'd be bothered. I was mostly able to put it out of my mind. One of the few things left in the world, aside from the world itself, that sadden me every day is an awareness that you get upset if Boo Boo or Walt tells you you're saying something that sounds like me. You sort of take it as an accusation of piracy, a little slam at your individuality. Is it so bad that we sometimes sound like each other?

The membrane is so thin between us. Is it so important for us to keep in mind which is whose? That time two summers ago when I was out so long, I was able to trace that you and Z. and I have been brothers for no fewer than four incarnations, maybe more. Is there no beauty in that? For us, doesn't each of our individualities begin right at the point where we own up to our extremely close connections and accept the inevitability of borrowing one another's jokes, talents, idiocies? You notice I don't include neckties. I think Buddy's neckties are Buddy's neckties, but they *are* a pleasure to borrow without permission.

It must be terrible for you to think I have neckties and things on my mind besides your story. I don't. I'm just looking everywhere for my thoughts. I thought this trivia might help me to collect myself. It's daylight out, and I've been sitting here since you went to bed. What bliss it is to be your first reader. It would be straight bliss if I didn't think you valued my opinion more than your own. It really doesn't seem right to me that you should rely so heavily on my opinion of your stories. That is, *you*. You can argue me down another time, but I'm convinced I've done something very wrong that this situation should be. I'm not exactly wallowing in guilt at the moment, but guilt is guilt. It doesn't go away. It can't be nullified. It can't even be fully understood, I'm certain – its roots run too deep into private and long-standing karma. About the only thing that saves my neck when I get to feeling this way is that guilt is an imperfect form of knowledge. Just because it isn't perfect doesn't mean that it can't be used. The hard thing to do is to put it to practical use before it gets around to paralyzing you. So I'm going to write down what I think about this story as fast as I can. If I hurry, I have a powerful feeling my guilt will serve the best and truest purposes here. I do think that. I think if I rush with this, I may be able to tell you what I've probably wanted to tell you for years.

You must know yourself that this story is full of big jumps. Leaps. When you first went to bed, I thought for a while that I ought to wake up everybody in the house and throw a party for our marvellous jumping brother. What *am* I, that I didn't wake everybody up? I wish I knew. A worrier, at the very best. I worry about big jumps that I can measure off with my eyes. I think I dream of your daring to jump right out of my sight. Excuse this. I'm writing very fast now. I think this new story is the one you've been waiting for. And me, too, in a way. You know it's mostly *pride* that's keeping me up. I think that's my main worry. For your own sake, don't make me proud of you. I think that's exactly what I'm trying to say. If only you'd never keep me up again out of pride. Give me a story that just makes me unreasonably vigilant. *Keep me up till five only because all your stars are out, and for no other reason.* Excuse the underlining, but that's the first thing I've ever said about one of your stories that makes my head go up and down. Please don't let me say anything else. I think tonight that anything you say to a writer after you beg him to let his stars come out is just literary advice. I'm positive tonight that all 'good' literary advice is just Louis Bouilhet and Max Du Camp wishing Madame Bovary on Flaubert. All right, so between the two of them, with their exquisite taste, they got him to write a masterpiece. They killed his chances of ever writing his heart out. He died like a celebrity, which was the one thing he wasn't. His letters are unbearable to read. They're so much better than they should be. They read waste, waste, waste. They break my heart. I dread saying anything to you tonight, dear old Buddy, except the trite. Please follow your heart, win or lose. You got so mad at me when we were registering. [*The week before, he and I and several million other young Americans went over to the nearest public school and registered for the draft. I caught him smiling at something I had written on my registration blank. He declined, all the way home, to tell me what struck him so funny. As anyone in my family could verify, he could be an inflexible decliner when the occasion looked auspicious to him.*] Do you know what I was smiling at? You wrote down that you were a writer by *profession*. It sounded to me like the loveliest euphemism I had ever heard. When was writing ever your profession? It's never been anything but your religion. Never. I'm a little over-excited now. Since it *is* your religion, do you know what you will be asked when you die? But let me tell you first what you won't be asked. You won't be asked if you were working on a wonderful, moving piece of writing when you died. You won't be asked if it was long or short, sad or funny, published or unpublished. You won't be asked if you were in good or bad form while you were working on it. You won't even be asked if it was the one piece of writing you would have been working on if you had known your time would be up when it was finished – I think only poor Sören K. will get asked that. I'm so sure you'll get asked only two questions. *Were most of your stars out? Were you busy writing your heart out?* If only you knew how easy it would be for you to say yes to both questions. If only you'd remember before ever you sit down to write that you've been a *reader* long before you were ever a writer. You simply fix that fact in your mind, then sit very still and ask yourself, as a reader, what piece of writing in all the world Buddy Glass would most want to read if he had his heart's choice. The next step is terrible, but so simple I can hardly believe it as I write it. You just sit down shamelessly and write the thing yourself. I won't even underline that. It's too important to be underlined. Oh, dare to do it, Buddy! Trust your heart. You're a deserving craftsman. It would never betray you. Good night, I'm feeling very much over-excited now, and a little dramatic, but I think I'd give almost anything on earth to see you writing a something, an anything, a story, a poem, a tree, that was really and truly after your own heart. The Bank Dick is at the Thalia. Let's take the whole bunch tomorrow night. Love, S.

This is Buddy Glass back on the page. (Buddy Glass, of course, is only my pen name. My *real* name is Major George Fielding Anti-Climax.) I'm feeling over-excited and a little dramatic myself, and my every heated impulse at this second is to make literally starry promises to the reader for our rendezvous tomorrow night. But if I'm smart, I think, I'll just brush my tooth and run along to bed. If my brother's long Memo was rather taxing to read, it was positively exhausting, I can't forbear to add, to type out for my friends. At this moment, I'm wearing that handsome firmament he offered me as a hurry-up-and-get-well-from-your-hepatitis-and-faintheartedness present down around my knees.

Will it be too rash of me, though, to tell the reader what I intend to do, beginning tomorrow night? For ten years and more, I've dreamed of having the question 'What did your brother Look Like?' put to me by someone with no special preference for brief, *crisp* answers to very direct questions. In short, the piece of writing in this world, 'the something, the anything,' that my recommended organ of authority tells me I'd most enjoy curling up with is a full physical description of Seymour written by somebody who isn't in an all-fired hurry to get him off his chest – in a properly shameless word, myself.

His hair jumping in the barbershop. This is Tomorrow Night, and I'm sitting here, it goes without saying, in my tuxedo. *His hair jumping in the barbershop.* Jesus God, is that my opening line? Is this room going to fill up, slowly, slowly, with corn muffins and apple pie? It may. I don't want to believe it, but it may. If I push for Selectiveness with a description, I'll quit cold again before I start. I can't sort out, can't clerk with this man. I can hope that *some* things will be bound to get done here with passing sensibility, but let me not screen every damned sentence, for once in my life, or I'm through again. His jumping hair in the barbershop is absolutely the first pressing thing that comes to mind. We went for haircuts usually every second broadcast day, or once every two weeks, right after school was out. The barbershop was at 108th and Broadway, nested verdantly (stop that, now) between a Chinese restaurant and a kosher delicatessen. If we'd forgotten to eat lunch, or, more likely, *lost* it somewhere, we sometimes bought about fifteen cents' worth of sliced salami and a couple of new dill pickles, and ate them in our chairs, at least till the hair started to fall. Mario and Victor were the barbers. Probably passed on, these many years, of an overdose of garlic, the way all New York barbers eventually go. (All right, *cut that out*. Just manage to nip that stuff in the bud, please.) Our chairs were adjoining, and when Mario had finished with me and was ready to take off and shake out that cloth throwover, I never, never failed to have more of Seymour's hair on me than my own. Few things in my life, before or since, have riled me more. Only once did I put in a complaint about it, and that was a colossal mistake. I said something, in a distinctly ratty tone of voice, about his 'damn hair' always jumping all over me. The instant I said it I was sorry, but it was out. He didn't say anything, but he immediately started to *worry* about it. It grew worse as we walked home, crossing streets in silence; he was obviously trying to divine a way of forbidding his hair to jump on his brother in the barbershop. The homestretch on 110th, the long block from Broadway to our building, on the corner of Riverside, was the worst. No one in the family could worry his or her way down that block the way Seymour could if he had Decent Material.

Which is enough for one night. I'm exhausted.

Just this one other thing. What is it I *want* (italics all mine) from a physical description of him? More, what do I want it to *do*? I want it to get to the magazine, yes; I want to publish it. But that isn't it – I *always* want to publish. It has more to do with the *way* I want to submit it to the magazine. In fact, it has everything to do with that. I think I know. I know very well I know. I want it to get down there without my using either stamps or a Manila envelope. If it's a true description, I should be able to just give it it's train fare, and maybe pack a sandwich for it and a little something hot in a thermos, and that's all. The other passengers in the car must move slightly away from it, as though it were a trifle high. Oh, marvellous thought! *Let him come out of this a trifle high.* But what kind of high? High, I think, like someone you love coming up on the porch, grinning, grinning, after three hard sets of tennis, *victorious* tennis, to ask you if you saw that last shot he made. Yes. *Oui.*

Another night. This is to be read, remember. Tell the reader where you are. Be friendly – *you never know*. But of course. I'm in the conservatory, I've just rung for the port, and it will be brought in at any moment by the old family retainer, an exceptionally intelligent, fat, sleek mouse, who eats everything in the house except examination papers.

I'm going back to S.'s hair, since it's already on the page. Till it started coming out, at about nineteen, in handfuls, he had very wiry black hair. The word is almost kinky, but not quite; I think I'd feel determined to use it if it had been. It was most exceedingly pullable-looking hair, and pulled it surely got; the babies in the family always automatically reached for it, even before the nose, which, God wot, was also Outstanding. But one thing at a time. A very hairy man, youth, adolescent. The other kids in the family, not exclusively but especially the boys, the many pre-puberty boys we always seemed to have around the house, used to be fascinated by his wrists and hands. My brother Walt, at about eleven, had a routine of looking at Seymour's wrists and inviting him to take off his sweater. 'Take off your sweater, hey, Seymour. Go ahead, hey. It's *warm* in here.' S. would beam back at him, shine back at him. He loved that kind of horseplay from any of the kids. I did, too, but only off and on. He did invariably. He thrived, too, waxed strong, on all tactless or underconsidered remarks directed at him by family minors. In 1959, in fact, when on occasion I hear rather nettling news of the doings of my youngest brother and sister, I think on the quantities of joy they brought S. I remember Franny, at about four, sitting on his lap, facing him, and saying, with immense admiration, 'Seymour, your teeth are so nice and *yellow*!' He literally staggered over to me to ask if I'd heard what she said.

One remark in this last paragraph stops me cold. Why did I like horseplay from the kids only off and on? Undoubtedly because it sometimes had a fair amount of malice in it when it was directed at me. Not that I most probably didn't have it coming to me. What, I wonder, does the reader know of large families? More important, how much can he stand hearing on the subject, from me? I must say at least this much: If you're an older brother in a large family (particularly where, as with Seymour and Franny, there's an age difference of roughly eighteen years), and you either cast yourself or just not very advertently become cast in the role of local tutor or mentor, it's almost impossible not to turn into a monitor, too. But even monitors come in individual shapes, sizes, and colors. For example, when Seymour told one of the twins or Zooey or Franny, or even Mme Boo Boo (who was only two years younger than myself, and often entirely the Lady), to take off his or her rubbers on coming into the apartment, each and all of them knew he mostly meant that the floor would get tracked up if they didn't and that Bessie would have to get out the mop. When *I* told them to take off their rubbers, they knew I mostly meant that people who didn't were slobs. It was bound to make no small difference in the way they kidded or ragged us separately. A confession, I groan to overhear, that can't avoid sounding suspiciously Honest and Ingratiating. What can I do about it? Am I to hold up the whole works every time an Honest John tone comes into my voice? Can't I count on the reader's knowing that I wouldn't play myself down – in this instance, stress my poor leadership qualities – if I didn't feel certain that I was much more than lukewarmly tolerated in that house? Would it help to tell you my age again? I'm a gray-haired, flaccid-bottomed forty as I write this, with a fair-sized pot and some commensurately fair-sized chances, I hope, of not throwing my silver pusher on the floor because I'm not going to make the basketball squad this year or because my salute isn't snappy enough to send me to Officer Candidate School. Besides, a confessional passage has probably never been written that didn't stink a little bit of the writer's pride in having given up his pride. The thing to listen for, every time, with a public confessor, is what he's *not* confessing to. At a certain period of his life (usually, grievous to say, a *successful* period), a man may suddenly feel it Within His Power to confess that he cheated on his final exams at college, he may even choose to reveal that between the ages of twenty-two and twenty-four he was sexually impotent, but these gallant confessions in themselves are no guarantee that we'll find out whether he once got piqued at his pet hamster and stepped on its head. I'm sorry to go on about this, but it seems to me I have a legitimate worry here. I'm writing about the only person I've ever known whom, on my own terms, I considered really large, and the only person of *any* considerable dimensions I've ever known who never gave me a moment's suspicion that he kept, on the sly, a whole closetful of naughty, tiresome little vanities. I find it dreadful – in fact, sinister – even to have to wonder whether I may not occasionally be nosing him out in popularity on the page. You'll pardon me, maybe, for saying so, but not all readers are skilled readers. (When Seymour was twenty-one, a nearly full professor of English, and had already been teaching for two years, I asked him what, if anything, got him down about teaching. He said he didn't think that anything about it got him exactly *down*, but there was one thing, he thought, that frightened him: reading the pencilled notations in the margins of books in the college library.) I'll finish this. Not all readers, I repeat, are skilled readers, and I'm told – critics tell us *everything*, and the worst first – that I have many surface charms as a writer. I wholeheartedly fear that there is a type of reader who may find it somewhat winning of me to have lived to be forty; i.e., unlike Another Person on the page, not to have been 'selfish' enough to commit suicide and leave my Whole Loving Family high and dry. (I said I'd finish this, but I'm not going to make it after all. Not because I'm not a proper iron man but because to finish it right I'd have to touch on – my God, *touch on* – the details of his suicide, and I don't expect to be ready to do that, at the rate I'm going, for several more years.)

I'll tell you one thing, though, before I go to bed, that seems to me vastly pertinent. And I'd be grateful if everybody tried his hardest not to consider this a categorical afterthought. I can give you, that is, one perfectly explorable reason that makes my being forty at this writing a monstrous advantage-disadvantage. Seymour was dead at thirty-one. Even to bring him up to *that* exceedingly unhoary age will take me many, many months, as I'm geared, and probably years. For the present, you'll see him almost exclusively as a child and young boy (never, I hope to God, as a *nipper*). While I'm with him in the business on the page, I'll be a child and young boy, too. But always I'll be aware, and so, I believe, will the reader, if rather less partisanly, that a somewhat paunchy and very nearly middle-aged man is running this show. In my view, this thought is no more melancholy than most of the facts of life and death, but no less, either. You've only my word for it so far, but I must tell you that I know as well as I know anything that if our positions were switched around and Seymour were in my seat, he would be so affected – so stricken, in fact – by his gross seniority as narrator and official shot-caller that he'd abandon this project. I'll say no more about it, of course, but I'm glad it came up. It's the truth. Please don't simply see it; feel it.

I'm not going to bed after all. Somebody around here hath murdered sleep. Good for him.

Shrill, unpleasant voice (not of any of *my* readers): You said you were going to tell us what your brother Looked Like. We don't want all this goddam analysis and gluey stuff.

But I do. I want every bit of this gluey stuff. I could use a little less an*al*ysis, no doubt, but I want every bit of the gluey stuff. If I have a prayer of staying straight with this, it's the gluey stuff that'll do it.

I think I can describe his face, form, manner – the works – at almost any time of his life (barring the overseas years) and get a good likeness. No euphemisms, please. A perfect image. (When and where, if I go on with this, will I have to tell the reader what sort of memories, powers of recall, some of us in the family have? Seymour, Zooey, myself. I can't put it off indefinitely, but how ugly will it look in print?) It would help enormously if some kind soul were to send me a telegram stating precisely which Seymour he'd prefer me to describe. If I'm called upon merely to describe *Seymour*, any Seymour, I get a vivid-type picture, all right, but in it he appears before me simultaneously at the ages of, approximately, eight, eighteen, and twenty-eight, with a full head of hair and getting very bald, wearing a summer camper's red-striped shorts and wearing a creased suntan shirt with buck-sergeant stripes, sitting in padmasana and sitting in the balcony at the R.K.O. 86th Street. I feel the threat of presenting just that kind of picture, and I don't like it. For one thing, I think it would worry Seymour. It's rough when one's Subject is also one's *cher maître*. It wouldn't worry him a very great deal, I think, if after due consultation with my instincts I elected to use some sort of literary Cubism to present his face. For that matter, it wouldn't worry him at all if I wrote the rest of this exclusively in lower-case letters – *if* my instincts advised it. I wouldn't *mind* some form of Cubism here, but every last one of my instincts tells me to put up a good, lower-middle-class fight against it. I'd like to sleep on it, anyway. Good night. Good night, Mrs Calabash. Good night, Bloody Description.

Since I'm having a little trouble speaking for myself, I decided this morning, in class (rather staring the while, I'm afraid, at Miss Valdemar's incredibly snug pedal pushers), that the really courteous thing to do would be to let one of my parents have the first word here, and where better to start than with the Primeval Mother? The risks involved, though, are overwhelming. If sentiment doesn't ultimately make fibbers of some people, their natural abominable memories almost certainly will. With Bessie, for instance, one of the main things about Seymour was his tallness. In her mind she sees him as an uncommonly rangy, Texan type, forever ducking his head as he came into rooms. The fact is, he was five ten and a half – a short tall man by modern, multiple-vitamin standards. Which was fine with him. He had no love whatever for height. I wondered for a while, when the twins went over six feet, whether he was going to send them condolence cards. I think if he were alive today he'd be all smiles that Zooey, being an actor, grew up small. He, S., was a very firm believer in low centers of gravity for real actors.

That bit about 'all smiles' was a mistake. I can't get him to stop smiling now. I'd be very happy if some other earnest-type writer sat in for me here. One of my first vows when I took up this profession was to put the damper on my characters' Smiling or Grinning on the printed page. Jacqueline grinned. Big, lazy Bruce Browning smiled wryly. A boyish smile lit up Captain Mittagessen's craggy features. Yet it presses in on me like hell here. To get the worst over with first: I think he had a very, very good smile, for somebody whose teeth were somewhere between so-so and bad. What seems not a whit onerous to write about is the mechanics of it. His smile often went backward or forward when all the other facial traffic in the room was either not moving at all or moving in the opposite direction. His distributor wasn't standard, even in the family. He could look grave, not to say funereal, when candles on small children's birthday cakes were being blown out. On the other hand, he could look positively delighted when one of the kids showed him where he or she had scraped a shoulder swimming under the float. Technically, I think, he had no social smile whatever, and yet it seems true (maybe just a *trifle* extravagant) to say that nothing essentially right was ever missing in his face. His scraped-shoulder smile, for example, was often maddening, if it was *your* shoulder that had got scraped, but it also distracted where distraction counted. His gravity at birthday parties, surprise parties, didn't wet-blanket them – or almost never, any more than, say, his grinniness as a guest at First Communions or Bar Mizvahs. And I don't think this is just the prejudiced brother talking. People who didn't know him at all, or knew him only slightly, or just as a Child Radio Celebrity, active or retired, were sometimes *disconcerted* by a particular expression – or a lack of one – on his face, but merely for a moment, I think. And often in such cases the victims felt something pleasantly close to curiosity – never, that I can remember, any real personal resentment or ruffling of the feathers. For one reason – the least complex, surely – his every expression was ingenuous. When he was to manhood grown (and this *is*, I suppose, the prejudiced brother speaking), I think he had about the last absolutely unguarded adult face in the Greater New York Area. The only times I can remember anything disingenuous, artful, going on in his face were when he was intentionally amusing some blood relative around the apartment. Even this, though, wasn't a daily occurrence. On the whole, I'd say, he partook of Humor with a temperateness denied to anyone else in our household. Which, rather emphatically, is not to imply that humor wasn't a staple of his diet, too, but it is to say that he generally got, or took for himself, the smallest piece. The Standing Family Joke almost invariably fell to him, if our father wasn't around at the moment, and he usually put it away with good grace. For a neat enough example, I think, of what I mean, when I read my new short stories aloud to him it was his unwavering custom, once in every story, to interrupt me in the middle of a line of dialogue to ask me if I knew that I had a Good Ear for the Rhythms and Cadences of Colloquial Speech. It was his pleasure to look very sapient as he put that one to me.

What I get next is Ears. In fact, I get a whole little movie of them – a streaky one-reeler of my sister Boo Boo, at about eleven, leaving the dinner table on a riotous impulse and lunging back into the room a minute later to try out a pair of rings, detached from a loose-leaf notebook, on Seymour's ears. She was very pleased with the result, and Seymour kept them on all evening. Not improbably till they drew blood. But they weren't for him. He hadn't, I'm afraid, the ears of a buccaneer but the ears of an old cabalist or an old Buddha. Extremely long, fleshy lobes. I remember Father Waker, passing through here a few years ago in a hot black suit, asking me, while I was doing the *Times* crossword, if I thought S.'s ears had been Tang dynasty. Myself, I'd put it earlier than that.

I'm going to bed. Perhaps a nightcap, first, in the Library, with Colonel Anstruther, then bed. Why does this exhaust me so? The hands are sweating, the bowels churning. The Integrated Man is simply not at home.

Except for the eyes, and maybe (I say *maybe*) the nose, I'm tempted to pass up the rest of his face, and the hell with Comprehensiveness. I couldn't bear to be accused of leaving *nothing* to the reader's imagination.

In one or two conveniently describable ways, his eyes were similar to mine, to Les's, and to Boo Boo's, in that (a) the eyes of this bunch could all be rather bashfully described as extra-dark oxtail in color, or Plaintive Jewish Brown, and (b) we all ran to half circles, and, in a couple of cases, outright bags. There, though, all intra-familial comparison stops dead. It seems a little ungallant to the ladies of the ensemble, but my vote for the two 'best' pairs of eyes in the family would go to Seymour and Zooey. And yet each of those pairs was so utterly different from the other, and color only the least of it. A few years ago, I published an ex*cep*tionally Haunting, Memorable, unpleasantly controversial, and thoroughly unsuccessful short story about a 'gifted' little boy aboard a transatlantic liner, and somewhere in it there was a detailed description of the boy's eyes. By a happy stroke of coincidence, I happen to have a copy of that very story on my person at this moment, tastefully pinned to the lapel of my bathrobe. I quote: 'His eyes, which were pale brown in color and not at all large, were slightly crossed – the left eye more than the right. They were not crossed enough to be disfiguring, or even to be necessarily noticeable at first glance. They were crossed just enough to be mentioned, and only in context with the fact that one might have thought long and seriously before wishing them straighter, or deeper, or browner, or wider set.' (Perhaps we'd better pause a second to catch our *breath*.) The fact is (truly, no Ho Ho intended), those were not Seymour's eyes at all. His eyes were dark, very large, quite adequately spaced, and, if anything, exceedingly uncrossed. Yet at least two members of my family knew and remarked that I was trying to get at his eyes with that description, and even felt that I hadn't brought it off too badly, in a *peculiar* way. In reality, there was something like a here-again, gone-again, super-gossamer cast over his eyes – except that it wasn't a cast at all, and *that* was where I ran into trouble. Another, equally fun-loving writer – Schopenhauer – tries, somewhere in *his* hilarious work, to describe a similar pair of eyes, and makes, I'm delighted to say, an entirely comparable hash of it.

All right. The Nose. I tell myself this'll only hurt a minute.

If, any time between 1919 and 1948, you came into a crowded room where Seymour and I were present, there would possibly be only one way, but it would be foolproof, of knowing that he and I were brothers. That would be by the noses and chins. The chins, of course, I can breezily dismiss in a minute by saying we almost didn't have any. Noses, however, we emphatically had, and they were close to being identical: two great, fleshy, drooping, *trompe*-like affairs that were different from every other nose in the family except, all too vividly, that of dear old Great-Grandfather Zozo, whose own nose, ballooning out from an early daguerreotype, used to alarm me considerably as a small boy. (Come to think of it, Seymour, who never made, shall I say, anatomical jokes, once rather surprised me by wondering whether our noses – his, mine, Great-Grandfather Zozo's – posed the same bedtime dilemma that certain beards do, meaning did we sleep with them outside or inside the covers.) There's a risk, though, of sounding too *airy* about this. I'd like to make it very clear – offensively so, if need be – that they were definitely not romantic Cyrano protuberances. (Which is a dangerous subject on all counts, I think, in this brave new psychoanalytical world, where almost everybody as a matter of course knows which came first, Cyrano's nose or his wisecracks, and where there's a widespread, international clinical hush for all the big-nosed chaps who are undeniably tongue-tied.) I think the only difference worth mentioning in the general breadth, length, and contours of our two noses was that there was a very notable bend, I'm obliged to say, to the right, an extra lopsidedness, at the bridge of Seymour's nose. Seymour always suspected that it made my nose patrician by comparison. The 'bend' was acquired when someone in the family was rather dreamily making practice swings with a baseball bat in the hall of our old apartment on Riverside Drive. His nose was never set after the mishap.

Hurrah. The nose is over. I'm going to bed.

I don't dare look back yet over what I've written so far; the old occupational fear of turning into a used Royal typewriter ribbon at the stroke of midnight is *very* strong tonight. I have a good idea, though, that I haven't been presenting a living portrait of the Sheik of Arabee. Which is, I pray, fair and correct. At the same time, no one must be led to infer, through my damned incompetence and heat, that S. was, in the usual, tiresome terminology, an Attractively Ugly Man. (It's a very suspect tag in *any* event, most commonly used by certain womenfolk, real or imaginary, to justify their perhaps too singular attraction to spectacularly sweet-wailing demons or, somewhat less categorically, badly brought-up swans.) Even if I have to hammer at it – and I already have, I'm aware – I must make it plain that we were, if to slightly different degrees, two obtrusively 'homely' children. My God, were we homely. And though I think I may say that our looks 'improved considerably' with age and as our faces 'filled out,' I must assert and reassert that as boys, youths, adolescents, we undoubtedly gave a great many genuinely thoughtful people a distinct pang at first sight. I'm speaking here, of course, of adults, not other children. Most young children don't pang very readily – not that way, anyhow. On the other hand, neither are most young children notably large-hearted. Often, at children's parties, someone's rather showily broad-minded mother would suggest a game of Spin the Bottle or Post Office, and I can freely attest that throughout childhood the two eldest Glass boys were veteran recipients of bag after bag of unmailed letters (illogically but satisfactorily put, I think), unless, of course, the Postman was a little girl called Charlotte the Harlot, who was a trifle mad anyway. Did this bother us? Did it cause pain? *Think carefully, now, writer.* My very slow, very considered answer: Almost never. In my own case, for three reasons that I can easily think of. First, except for one or two shaky intervals, I believed straight through my childhood – thanks largely to Seymour's insistence, but by no means entirely – that I was an egregiously charming, able fellow, and it was at once a marked and a curiously unimportant reflection on anyone's taste if he thought otherwise. Second (if you can stand this one, and I don't see how you can), I had a rosy, full conviction before I was five that I was going to be a superlative writer when I grew up. And, third, with very few deviations, and none whatever within the heart, I was always secretly pleased and proud to bear any physical resemblance to Seymour. With Seymour himself, the case, as usual, was different. He cared alternately much and not at all about his funny-lookingness. When he cared much, he cared for the sake of other people, and I find myself thinking especially, at this moment, of our sister Boo Boo. Seymour was wild about her. Which isn't saying a great deal, since he was wild about everybody in the family and most people outside it. But, like all young girls *I've* ever known, Boo Boo went through a stage – admirably short, in her case, I must say – when she 'died' at least twice daily over the *gaffes*, the *faux pas*, of adults in general. At the height of this period, a favorite history teacher who came into class after lunch with a dot of charlotte russe on her cheek was quite sufficient cause for Boo Boo to wither and die at her desk. Quite frequently, however, she came home dead from somewhat less trivial causes, and these were the times that bothered and worried Seymour. He worried rather particularly, for her sake, about adults who came over to us (him and me) at parties or such to tell us how handsome we were looking tonight. If not that precisely, that *sort* of thing happened not seldom, and Boo Boo always seemed to be within earshot when it did, positively waiting to die.

Perhaps I feel less concerned than I ought to feel about the possibility of going overboard on this subject of his face, his *physical* face. I'll concede, readily, a certain absence of total perfection in my methods. Perhaps I'm overdoing this whole description. For one thing, I see that I've discussed almost every feature of his face and haven't so much as touched on the *life* of it yet. That thought in itself – I hadn't expected it – is a staggering depressant. Yet even while I feel it, even while I go under with it, a certain conviction that I've had from the beginning remains intact – snug and dry. 'Conviction' isn't the right word at all. It's more like a prize for the best glutton for punishment, or a certificate of endurance. I feel I have a *knowledge*, a kind of editorial insight gained from all my failures over the past eleven years to describe him on paper, and this knowledge tells me he cannot be got at with understatement. The contrary, in fact. I've written and histrionically burned at least a dozen stories or sketches about him since 1948 – some of them, and I says it what shouldn't, pretty snappy and readable. But they were not Seymour. Construct an understatement for Seymour and it turns, it *matures*, into a lie. An artistic lie, maybe, and sometimes, even, a delicious lie, but a lie.

I feel I should stay up for another hour or so. Turnkey! *See that this man doesn't go to bed.*

There was such a lot that wasn't gargoyle in the least. His hands, for instance, were very fine. I hesitate to say beautiful, because I don't want to run into the thoroughly damnable expression 'beautiful hands.' The palms were broad, the muscle between thumb and index finger unexpectedly developed-looking, 'strong' (the quotes are *unnecessary* – for God's sake, relax), and yet the fingers were longer and thinner than Bessie's, even; the middle fingers looked like something you would measure with a tailor's tape.

I'm thinking about this last paragraph. That is, about the amount of personal admiration that has gone into it. To what extent, I wonder, may one be allowed to admire one's brother's hands without raising a few modern eyebrows? In my youth, Father William, my heterosexuality (discounting a few, shall I say, not always quite voluntary slow periods) was often rather common gossip in some of my old Study Groups. Yet I now find myself recalling, perhaps just a wee bit too vividly, that Sofya Tolstoy, in one of her, I don't doubt, well-provoked marital piques, accused the father of her thirteen children, the elderly man who continued to inconvenience her every night of her married life, of homosexual leanings. I think, on the whole, Sofya Tolstoy was a remarkably unbrilliant woman – and my atoms, moreover, are arranged to make me constitutionally inclined to believe that where there's smoke there's usually strawberry Jello, seldom fire – but I do very emphatically believe there is an enormous amount of the androgynous in any all-or-nothing prose writer, or even a would-be one. I think that if he titters at male writers who wear invisible skirts he does so at his eternal peril. I'll say no more on the subject. This is precisely the sort of confidence that can be easily and juicily Abused. It's a wonder we're not worse cowards in print than we already are.

Seymour's speaking voice, his incredible voice box, I can't discuss right here. I haven't room to back up properly first. I'll just say, for the moment, in my own unattractive Mystery Voice, that his speaking voice was the best wholly imperfect musical instrument I've ever listened to by the hour. I repeat, though, I'd like to postpone going ahead with a full description of it.

His skin was dark, or at least on the very far, safe side of sallow, and it was extraordinarily clear. He went all through adolescence without a pimple, and this both puzzled and irritated me greatly, since he ate just about the same amount of pushcart fare – or what our mother called Unsanitary Food Made by Dirty Men That Never Even Wash Their Hands – that I did, drank at least as much bottled soda as I drank, and surely washed no more often than I did. If anything, he washed a lot less than I did. He was so busy seeing to it that the rest of the bunch – particularly the twins – bathed regularly that he often missed his own turn. Which snaps me, not very conveniently, right back to the subject of barbershops. As we were on our way to get haircuts one afternoon, he stopped dead short in the middle of Amsterdam Avenue and asked me, very soberly, with cars and trucks clipping past us from both directions, if I'd mind very much getting a haircut without him. I pulled him over to the curb (I'd like to have a nickel for every curb I pulled him over to, man and boy) and said I certainly *would* mind. He had a notion his neck wasn't clean. He was planning to spare Victor, the barber, the offense of looking at his dirty neck. It *was* dirty, properly speaking. This was neither the first nor the last time that he inserted a finger in the back of his shirt collar and asked me to take a look. Usually that area was as well policed as it ought to have been, but when it wasn't, it definitely wasn't.

I really must go to bed now. The Dean of Women – a very sweet person – is coming at the crack of dawn to vacuum.

The terrible subject of clothes should get in here somewhere. What a marvellous convenience it would be if writers could let themselves describe their characters' clothes, article by article, crease by crease. What stops us? In part, the tendency to give the reader, whom we've never met, either the short end or the benefit of the doubt – the short end when we don't credit him with knowing as much about men and mores as we do, the benefit when we prefer not to believe that he has the same kind of petty, sophisticated data at his fingertips that we have. For example, when I'm at my foot doctor's and I run across a photograph in *Peekaboo* magazine of a certain kind of up-and-coming American public personality – a movie star, a politician, a newly appointed college president – and the man is shown at home with a beagle at his feet, a Picasso on the wall, and himself wearing a Norfolk jacket, I'll usually be very nice to the dog and civil enough to the Picasso, but I can be intolerable when it comes to drawing conclusions about Norfolk jackets on American public figures. If, that is, I'm not taken with the particular personage in the first place, the jacket will cinch it. I'll assume from it that his horizons are widening just too goddam fast to suit me.

Let's *go*. As older boys, both S. and I were terrible dressers, each in his own way. It's a little odd (not really very) that we *were* such awful dressers, because as small boys we were quite satisfactorily and unremarkably turned out, I think. In the early part of our career as hired radio performers, Bessie used to take us down to De Pinna's, on Fifth Avenue, for our clothes. How she discovered that sedate and worthy establishment in the first place is almost anybody's guess. My brother Walt, who was a very elegant young man while he lived, used to feel that Bessie had simply gone up and asked a policeman. A not unreasonable conjecture, since our Bessie, when we were children, habitually took her knottiest problems to the nearest thing we had in New York to a Druidic oracle – the Irish traffic cop. In a way, I can suppose the reputed luck of the Irish *did* have something to do with Bessie's discovery of De Pinna's. But surely not everything, by a long shot. For instance (this is extraneous, but nice), my mother has never in any known latitude of the expression been a book-reader. Yet I've seen her go into one of the gaudy book palaces on Fifth Avenue to buy one of my nephews a birthday present and come out, emerge, with the Kay Nielsen-illustrated edition of *East of the Sun and West of the Moon,* and if you knew her, you'd be certain that she'd been Ladylike but aloof to cruising helpful salesmen. But let's go back to the way we looked as Youths. We started to buy our own clothes, independent of Bessie *and* of each other, when we were in our earliest teens. Being the older, Seymour was the first to branch out, as it were, but I made up for lost time when my chance came. I remember dropping Fifth Avenue like a cold potato when I had just turned fourteen, and making straight for Broadway – specifically, to a shop in the Fifties where the sales force, I thought, were more than faintly hostile but at least knew a born snappy dresser when they saw one coming. In the last year S. and I were on the air together – 1933 – I showed up every broadcast night wearing a pale-gray double-breasted suit with heavily wadded shoulders, a midnight-blue shirt with a Hollywood 'roll' collar, and the cleaner of two identical crocus-yellow cotton neckties I kept for formal occasions in general. I've never felt as good in anything since, frankly. (I don't suppose a writing man ever really gets rid of his old crocus-yellow neckties. Sooner or later, I think, they show up in his prose, and there isn't a hell of a lot he can do about it.) Seymour, on the other hand, picked out marvellously orderly clothes for himself. The main hitch *there* was that nothing he bought – suits, overcoats particularly – ever fitted him properly. He must have bolted, possibly half dressed, and certainly unchalked, whenever anyone from the alteration department approached him. His jackets all hiked either up or down on him. His sleeves usually either extended to the middle joints of his thumbs or stopped at the wristbones. The seats of his trousers were always close to the worst. They were sometimes rather awe-inspiring, as if a 36-Regular behind had been dropped like a pea in a basket into a 42-Long pair of trousers. But there are other and more formidable aspects to be considered here. Once an article of clothing was actually on his body, he lost all earthly consciousness of it – barring, perhaps, a certain vague technical awareness that he was no longer stark naked. And this wasn't simply a sign of an instinctive, or even a well-educated, anti pathy to being what was known in our circles as a Good Dresser. I did go along with him once or twice when he was Buying, and I think, looking back, that he bought his clothes with a mild but, to me, gratifying degree of pride – like a young *brahmacharya*, or Hindu-religious novice, picking out his first loincloth. Oh, it was a very odd business. Something always went wrong, too, with Seymour's clothes at the exact instant he was actually putting them on. He could stand for a good, normal three or four minutes in front of an open closet door surveying his side of our necktie rack, but you *knew* (if you were damned fool enough to sit around watching him) that once he'd actually made his selection the tie was doomed. Either its knot-to-be was fated to balk at fitting snugly into the V of his shirt collar – it most often came to rest about a quarter of an inch short of the throat button – or if the potential knot *was* to be slid safely into its proper place, then a little band of foulard was definitely fated to stick out from under the collar fold at the back of his neck, looking rather like a tourist's binoculars strap. But I'd prefer to leave this large and difficult subject. His clothes, in short, often wore the whole family to something akin to despair. I've given only a very *passing* description, really. The thing came in any number of variations. I might just add, and then drop it quickly, that it can be a deeply disturbing experience to be standing, say, beside one of the potted palms at the Biltmore, at cocktail rush hour, on a summer day, and have your liege lord come bounding up the public stairs obviously pleased as punch to see you but not entirely battened down, fastened.

I'd love to pursue this stairs-bounding business for a minute – that is, pursue it blind, without giving a great damn where it lands me. He bounded up all flights of stairs. He rushed them. I rarely saw him take a flight of stairs any other way. Which delivers me up – pertinently, I'm going to assume – to the subject of vim, vigor, and vitality. I can't imagine anyone, these days (I can't *easily* imagine anyone these days) – with the possible exception of unusually insecure longshoremen, a few retired general officers of the Army and Navy, and a great many small boys who worry about the size of their biceps – taking much stock in the old popular aspersions of Unrobustness laid to poets. Nonetheless, I'm prepared to suggest (particularly since so many military and outdoorsy thoroughgoing he-men number me among their favorite yarn spinners) that a very considerable amount of sheer physical stamina, and not merely nervous energy or a cast-iron ego, is required to get through the final draft of a first-class poem. Only too often, sadly, a good poet turns into a damned poor keeper of his body, but I believe he is usually issued a highly serviceable one to start out with. My brother was the most nearly tireless person I've known. (I'm suddenly time-conscious. It's not yet midnight, and I'm playing with the idea of sliding to the floor and writing this from a supine position.) It's just struck me that I never saw Seymour yawn. He must have, of course, but I never saw him. Surely not for any reasons of etiquette, either; yawns weren't fastidiously suppressed at home. I yawned regularly, I know – and I got more sleep than he did. Emphatically, though, we were both short sleepers, even as small boys. During, especially, our middle years on radio – the years, that is, when we each carried at least three library cards around with us in our hip pockets, like man-handled old passports – there were very few nights, *school* nights, when our bedroom lights went out before two or three in the morning, except during the crucial little post-Taps interval when First Sergeant Bessie was making her general rounds. When Seymour was hot on something, investigating something, he could and frequently did, from the age of about twelve, go two and three nights in a row without going to bed at all, and without distinctly looking or sounding the worse for it. Much loss of sleep apparently affected just his circulation; his hands and feet got cold. Along about the third wakeful night in a row, he'd look up at least once from whatever he was doing and ask me if I felt a terrible draft. (No one in our family, not even Seymour, felt drafts. Only terrible drafts.) Or he'd get up from the chair or the floor – wherever he was reading or writing or contemplating – and check to see if someone had left the bathroom window open. Besides me, Bessie was the only one in the apartment who could tell when Seymour was ignoring sleep. She judged by how many pairs of socks he was wearing. In the years after he'd graduated from knickers to long trousers, Bessie was forever lifting up the cuffs of his trousers to see if he was wearing two pairs of draftproof socks.

I'm my own Sandman tonight. Good night! Good night, all you infuriatingly uncommunicative people!

Many, many men my age and in my income bracket who write about their dead brothers in enchanting semi-diary form never even bother to give us dates or tell us where they *are*. No sense of collaboration. I've vowed not to let that happen to me. This is Thursday, and I'm back in my horrible chair.

It's a quarter to one in the morning, and I've been sitting here since ten, trying, while the physical Seymour is on the page, to find a way to introduce him as Athlete and Gamesman without excessively irritating anybody who hates sports and games. I'm dismayed and disgusted, really, to find I can't get into it unless I start with an apology. For one reason, I happen to belong to an English Department of which at least two members are well on their way to becoming established repertory modern poets and a third member is a literature critic of enormous chic here on the academic Eastern Seaboard, a rather towering figure among Melville specialists. All three of these men (they have great soft spots for me, too, as you might imagine) make what I tend to regard as a somewhat too public rush at the height of the professional-baseball season for a television set and a bottle of cold beer. Unfortunately, this small, ivy-covered stone is a little less devastating for the circumstance that I throw it from a solid-glass house. I've been a baseball fan myself all my life, and I don't doubt that there's an area inside my skull that must look like a bird-cage bottom of old shredded Sports Sections. In fact (and I consider this the last word in intimate writer-reader relations), probably one of the reasons I stayed on the air for well over six consecutive years as a child was that I could tell the Folks in Radioland what the Waner boys had been up to all week or, still more impressive, how many times Cobb had stolen third in 1921, when I was two. Am I still a trifle touchy about it? Have I still not made my peace with the afternoons of youth when I fled Reality, via the Third Avenue 'L,' to get to my little womb off third base at the Polo Grounds? I can't believe it. Maybe it's partly because I'm forty and I think it's high time all the elderly boy writers were asked to move along from the ballparks and the bull rings. No. I *know* – my God, I *know* – why I'm so hesitant to present the Aesthete as Athlete. I haven't thought of this in years and years, but this is the answer: There used to be an exceptionally intelligent and likable boy on the radio with S. and me – one Curtis Caulfield, who was eventually killed during one of the landings in the Pacific. He trotted off with Seymour and me to Central Park one afternoon, where I discovered he threw a ball as if he had two left hands – like most girls, in short – and I can still see the look on Seymour's face at the sound of my critical horse-laugh, stallion-laugh. (How can I explain away this deep-type analysis? Have I gone over to the Other Side? Should I hang out my shingle?)

Out with it. S. *loved* sports and games, indoors or outdoors, and was himself usually spectacularly good or spectacularly bad at them – seldom anything in between. A couple of years ago, my sister Franny informed me that one of her Earliest Memories is of lying in a 'bassinet' (like an Infanta, I gather) and watching Seymour play ping-pong with someone in the living room. In reality, I think, the bassinet she has in mind was a battered old crib on casters that her sister Boo Boo used to push her around in, all over the apartment, bumping her over doorsills, till the center of activity was reached. It's more than possible, though, that she did watch Seymour play ping-pong when she was an infant, and his unremembered and apparently colorless opponent could easily have been myself. I was generally dazed into complete colorlessness when I played ping-pong with Seymour. It was like having Mother Kali herself on the other side of the net, multi-armed and grinning, and without a particle of interest in the score. He banged, he chopped, he went after every second or third ball as though it were a lob and duly smashable. Roughly three out of five of Seymour's shots either went into the net or way the hell off the table, so it was virtually a volleyless game you played with him.

This was a fact, though, that never quite caught his undivided attention, and he was always surprised and abjectly apologetic when his opponent at length complained loudly and bitterly about chasing his balls all over the goddam room, under chairs, couch, piano, and in those nasty places behind shelved books.

He was equally crashing, and equally atrocious, at tennis. We played *often*. Especially my senior year in college, in New York. He was already teaching at the same institution, and there were many days, especially in spring, when I dreaded conspicuously fair weather, because I knew some young man would fall at my feet, like the Minstrel Boy, with a note from Seymour saying wasn't it a marvellous day and what about a little tennis later. I refused to play with him on the university courts, where I was afraid some of my friends *or* his – especially some of his fishier *Kollegen* – might spot him in action, and so we usually went down to Rip's Courts, on Ninety-sixth Street, an old hangout of ours. One of the most impotent stratagems I've ever devised was to deliberately keep my tennis racket and sneakers at home, rather than in my locker on campus. It had one small virtue, though. I usually got a modicum of sympathy while I was dressing to meet him on the courts, and not infrequently one of my sisters or brothers trooped compassionately to the front door with me to help me wait for the elevator.

At all card games, without exception – Go Fish, poker, cassino, hearts, old maid, auction or contract, slapjack, blackjack – he was absolutely intolerable. The Go Fish games were *watchable*, however. He used to play with the twins when they were small, and he was continually dropping hints to them to ask him if he had any fours or jacks, or elaborately coughing and exposing his hand. At poker, too, he was stellar. I went through a short period in my late teens when I played a semi-private, strenuous, losing game of turning into a good mixer, a regular guy, and I had people in frequently to play poker. Seymour often sat in on these sessions. It took some effort not to know when he was loaded with aces, because he'd sit there grinning, as my sister put it, like an Easter Bunny with a whole basketful of eggs. Worse still, he had a habit of holding a straight or a full house, or better, and then not raising, or even calling, somebody he liked across the table who was playing along with a pair of tens.

He was a lemon at four out of five outdoor sports. During our elementary-school days, when we lived at 110th and the Drive, there was usually a choose-up game of some kind going on in the afternoon, either on the side streets (stickball, roller-skate hockey) or, more often, on a patch of grass, a fair-sized dog run, near the statue of Kossuth, on Riverside Drive (football or soccer). At soccer or hockey, Seymour had a way, singularly unendearing to his teammates, of charging downfield – often brilliantly – and then stalling to give the opposing goalie time to set himself in an impregnable position. Football he very seldom played, and almost never unless one team or the other was short a man. I played it constantly. I didn't dislike violence, I was mostly just scared to death of it, and so had no real choice but to play; I even organized the damned games. On the few occasions when S. joined the football games, there was no way of guessing beforehand whether he was going to be an asset or a liability to his teammates. More often than not, he was the first boy picked in a choose-up game, because he was definitely snaky-hipped and a natural ballcarrier. If, in midfield, when he was carrying the ball, he didn't suddenly elect to give his heart to an oncoming tackler, he was a distinct asset to his side. As I say, though, there was no real telling, ever, whether he'd help or hinder the cause. Once, at one of the very rare and savory moments when my own teammates grudgingly allowed me to take the ball around one of the ends, Seymour, playing for the opposite side, disconcerted me by looking overjoyed to see me as I charged in his direction, as though it were an unexpected, an enormously providential chance encounter. I stopped almost dead short, and someone, of course, brought me down, in neighborhood talk, like a ton of bricks.

I'm going on too long about this, I know, but I really can't stop now. As I've said, he could be spectacularly good at certain games, too. Unpardonably so, in fact. By that I mean there is a degree of excellence in games or sports that we especially resent seeing reached by an unorthodox opponent, a categorical 'bastard' of some kind – a Formless Bastard, a Showy Bastard, or just a plain hundred-percent American bastard, which, of course, runs the gamut from somebody who uses cheap or inferior equipment against us with great success all the way down the line to a winning contestant who has an unnecessarily happy, good face. Only one of Seymour's crimes, when he excelled at games, was Formlessness, but it was a major one. I'm thinking of three games especially: stoopball, curb marbles, and pocket pool. (Pool I'll have to discuss another time. It wasn't just a game with us, it was almost a protestant reformation. We shot pool before or after almost every important crisis of our young manhood.) Stoopball, for the information of rural readers, is a ball game played with the support of a flight of brownstone steps or the front of an apartment building. As we played it, a rubber ball was thrown against some architectural granite fancywork – a popular Manhattan mixture of Greek Ionic and Roman Corinthian molding – along the façade of our apartment house, about waist-high. If the ball rebounded into the street or over to the far sidewalk and wasn't caught on the fly by someone on the opposing team, it counted as an infield hit, as in baseball; if it was caught – and this was more usual than not – the player was counted out. A home run was scored only when the ball sailed just high and hard enough to strike the wall of the building across the street without being caught on the bounce-off. In our day, quite a few balls used to reach the opposite wall on the fly, but very few fast, low, and choice enough so that they couldn't be handled on the fly. Seymour scored a home run nearly every time he was up. When other boys on the block scored one, it was generally regarded as a fluke – pleasant or unpleasant, depending on whose team you were on – but Seymour's failures to get home runs looked like flukes. Still more singular, and rather more to the point of this discussion, he threw the ball like no one else in the neighborhood. The rest of us, if we were normally right-handed, as *he* was, stood a little to the left of the ripply striking surfaces and let fly with a hard sidearm motion. Seymour *faced* the crucial area and threw straight *down* at it – a motion very like his unsightly and abominably unsuccessful overhand smash at ping-pong or tennis – and the ball zoomed back over his head, with a minimum of ducking on his part, straight for the bleachers, as it were. If you tried doing it his way (whether in private or under his positively zealous personal instruction), either you made an easy out or the (goddam) ball flew back and stung you in the face. There came a time when no one on the block would play stoopball with him – not even myself. Very often, then, he either spent some time explaining the fine points of the game to one of our sisters or turned it into an exceedingly effective game of solitaire, with the rebound from the opposite building lining back to him in such a way that he didn't have to change his footing to catch it on the trickle-in. (Yes, yes, I'm making too damned much of this, but I find the whole business irresistible, after nearly thirty years.) He was the same kind of heller at curb marbles. In curb marbles, the first player rolls or pitches his marble, his shooter, twenty or twenty-five feet along the edge of a side street where there are no cars parked, keeping his marble quite close to the curb. The second player then tries to hit it, shooting from the same starting line. It was rarely done, since almost anything could deflect a marble from going straight to its mark: the unsmooth street itself, a bad bounce against the curb, a wad of chewing gum, any one of a hundred typical New York side-street droppings – not to mention just plain, everyday lousy aim. If the second player missed with his first shot, his marble usually came to rest in a very vulnerable, close position for the first player to shoot at on his second turn. Eighty or ninety times out of a hundred, at this game, whether he shot first or last, Seymour was unbeatable. On long shots, he curved his marble at yours in a rather wide arc, like a bowling shot from the far-right side of the foul line. Here, too, his stance, his form, was maddeningly irregular. Where everybody else on the block made his long shot with an underhand toss, Seymour dispatched *his* marble with a sidearm – or, rather, a sidewrist – flick, vaguely like someone scaling a flat stone over a pond. And again imitation was disastrous. To do it his way was to lose all chance of *any* effective control over the marble.

I think a part of my mind has been vulgarly laying for this next bit. I haven't thought of it in years and years.

One late afternoon, at that faintly soupy quarter of an hour in

New York when the street lights have just been turned on and the parking lights of cars are just getting turned on – some on, some still off – I was playing curb marbles with a boy named Ira Yankauer, on the farther side of the side street just opposite the canvas canopy of our apartment house. I was eight. I was using Seymour's technique, or trying to – his side flick, his way of widely curving his marble at the other guy's – and I was losing steadily. Steadily but painlessly. For it was the time of day when New York City boys are much like Tiffin, Ohio, boys who hear a distant train whistle just as the last cow is being driven into the barn. At that magic quarter hour, if you lose marbles, you lose just marbles. Ira, too, I think, was properly time-suspended, and if so, all he could have been winning was marbles. Out of this quietness, and entirely in key with it, Seymour called to me. It came as a pleasant shock that there was a third person in the universe, and to this feeling was added the justness of its being Seymour. I turned around, totally, and I suspect Ira must have, too. The bulby bright lights had just gone on under the canopy of our house. Seymour was standing on the curb edge before it, facing us, balanced on his arches, his hands in the slash pockets of his sheep-lined coat. With the canopy lights behind him, his face was shadowed, dimmed out. He was ten. From the way he was balanced on the curb edge, from the position of his hands, from – well, the quantity *x* itself, I knew as well then as I know now that he was immensely conscious himself of the magic hour of the day. 'Could you try not aiming so much?' he asked me, still standing there. 'If you hit him when you aim, it'll just be luck.' He was speaking, communicating, and yet not breaking the spell. *I* then broke it. Quite deliberately. 'How can it be *luck* if I *aim*?' I said back to him, not loud (despite the italics) but with rather more irritation in my voice than I was actually feeling. He didn't say anything for a moment but simply stood balanced on the curb, looking at me, I knew imperfectly, with love. 'Because it will be,' he said. 'You'll be *glad* if you hit his marble – Ira's marble – won't you? Won't you be *glad*? And if you're *glad* when you hit somebody's marble, then you sort of secretly didn't expect too much to do it. So there'd have to be some luck in it, there'd have to be slightly quite a lot of *ac*cident in it.' He stepped down off the curb, his hands still in the slash pockets of his coat, and came over to us. But a thinking Seymour didn't cross a twilit street quickly, or surely didn't seem to. In that light, he came toward us much like a sailboat. Pride, on the other hand, is one of the fastest-moving things in this world, and before he got within five feet of us, I said hurriedly to Ira, 'It's getting dark anyway,' effectively breaking up the game.

This last little pentimento, or whatever it is, has started me sweating literally from head to foot. I want a cigarette, but my pack is empty, and I don't feel up to leaving this chair. Oh, God, what a noble profession this is. How well do I know the reader? How much can I tell him without unnecessarily embarrassing either of us? I can tell him this: A place has been prepared for each of us in his own mind. Until a minute ago, I'd seen mine four times during my life. This is the fifth time. I'm going to stretch out on the floor for a half hour or so. I beg you to excuse me.

This sounds to me very suspiciously like a playbill note, but after that last, theatrical paragraph I feel I have it coming to me. The time is three hours later. I fell asleep on the floor. (*I'm quite myself again, dear Baroness. Dear me, what* can *you have thought of me? You'll allow me, I beg of you, to ring for a rather interesting little bottle of wine. It's from my own little vineyards, and I think you* might *just . . .*) I'd like to announce – as briskly as possible – that whatever it precisely was that caused the Disturbance on the page three hours ago, I was not, am not now, and never have been the least bit intoxicated by my own powers (my own little powers, dear Baroness) of almost total recall. At the instant that I became, or made of myself, a dripping wreck, I was not strictly mindful of what Seymour was saying – or of Seymour himself, for that matter. What essentially struck me, incapacitated me, I think, was the sudden realization that Seymour is my Davega bicycle. I've been waiting most of my life for even the faintest inclination, let alone the follow-through required, to give away a Davega bicycle. I rush, of course, to explain:

When Seymour and I were fifteen and thirteen, we came out of our room one night to listen, I believe, to Stoopnagle and Budd on the radio, and we walked into a great and very ominously hushed commotion in the living room. There were only three people present – our father, our mother, and our brother Waker – but I have a notion there were other, smaller folk eavesdropping from concealed vantage points. Les was rather horribly flushed, Bessie's lips were compressed almost out of existence, and our brother Waker – who was at that instant, according to my figures, almost exactly nine years and fourteen hours old – was standing near the piano, in his pajamas, barefooted, with tears streaming down his face. My own first impulse in a family situation of that sort was to make for the hills, but since Seymour didn't look at all ready to leave, I stuck around, too. Les, with partly suppressed heat, at once laid the case for the prosecution before Seymour, That morning, as we already knew, Waker and Walt had been given matching, beautiful, well-over-the-budget birthday presents – two red-and-white striped, double-barred twenty-six-inch bicycles, the very vehicles in the window of Davega's Sports Store, on Eighty-sixth between Lexington and Third, that they'd both been pointedly admiring for the better part of a year. About ten minutes before Seymour and I came out of the bedroom, Les had found out that Waker's bicycle wasn't safely stored in the basement of our apartment building with Walt's. That afternoon, in Central Park, Waker had given his away. An unknown boy ('some shnook he never saw before in his *life*') had come up to Waker and asked him for his bicycle, and Waker had handed it over. Neither Les nor Bessie, of course, was unmindful of Waker's 'very nice, generous intentions,' but both of them also saw the details of the transaction with an implacable logic of their own. What, substantially, they felt that Waker should have done – and Les now repeated this opinion, with great vehemence, for Seymour's benefit – was to give the boy a nice, long *ride* on the bicycle. Here Waker broke in, sobbing. The boy didn't *want* a nice, long ride, he wanted the *bicycle*. He'd never *had* one, the boy; he'd always *wanted* one. I looked at Seymour. He was getting excited. He was acquiring a look of well-meaning but absolute inaptitude for arbitrating a difficult dispute of this kind – and I knew, from experience, that peace in our living room was about to be restored, however miraculously. ('The sage is full of anxiety and indecision in undertaking anything, and so he is always successful.' – Book XXVI, The Texts of Chuang-tzu.) I won't describe in detail (for once) how Seymour – and there must be a better way of putting this, but I don't know it – competently blundered his way to the heart of the matter so that, a few minutes later, the three belligerents actually kissed and made up. My real point here is a blatantly personal one, and I think I've already stated it.

What Seymour called over to me – or, rather, coached over to me – that evening at curb marbles in 1927 seems to me contributive and important, and I think I must certainly discuss it a little. Even though, somewhat shocking to say, almost nothing seems more contributive and important in my eyes at this interval than the fact of Seymour's flatulent brother, aged forty, at long last being presented with a Davega bicycle of his own to give away, preferably to the first asker. I find myself wondering, *musing*, whether it's quite *correct* to pass on from one pseudo-metaphysical fine point, however puny or personal, to another, however robust or impersonal. That is, without first lingering, lolling around a bit, in the wordy style to which I'm accustomed. Nonetheless, here goes: When he was coaching me, from the curbstone across the street, to quit aiming my marble at Ira Yankauer's – and he was ten, please remember – I believe he was instinctively getting at something very close in spirit to the sort of instructions a master archer in Japan will give when he forbids a willful new student to aim his arrows at the target; that is, when the archery master permits, as it were, Aiming but no aiming. I'd much prefer, though, to leave Zen archery and Zen itself out of this pint-size dissertation – partly, no doubt, because Zen is rapidly becoming a rather smutty, cultish word to the discriminating ear, and with great, if superficial, justification. (I say superficial because pure Zen will surely survive its Western champions, who, in the main, appear to confound its near-doctrine of Detachment with an invitation to spiritual indifference, even callousness – and who evidently don't hesitate to knock a Buddha down without first growing a golden fist. Pure Zen, need I add – and I think I do need, at the rate I'm going – will be here even after snobs like me have departed.) Mostly, however, I would prefer not to compare Seymour's marble-shooting advice with Zen archery simply because I am neither a Zen archer nor a Zen Buddhist, much less a Zen adept. (Would it be out of order for me to say that both Seymour's and my roots in Eastern philosophy – if I may hesitantly call them roots – were, are, planted in the New and Old Testaments, Advaita Vedanta, and classical Taoism? I tend to regard myself, if at all by anything as sweet as an Eastern name, as a fourth-class Karma Yogin, with perhaps a little Jnana Yoga thrown in to spice up the pot. I'm profoundly attracted to classical Zen literature, I have the gall to lecture on it and the literature of Mahayana Buddhism one night a week at college, but my life itself couldn't very conceivably be less Zenful than it is, and what little I've been able to apprehend – I pick that verb with care – of the Zen experience has been a by-result of following my own rather natural path of extreme Zenlessness. Largely because Seymour himself literally begged me to do so, and I never knew him to be wrong in these matters.) Happily for me, and probably for everybody, I don't believe it's really necessary to bring Zen into this. The method of marble-shooting that Seymour, by sheer intuition, was recommending to me can be related, I'd say, legitimately and un-Easternly, to the fine art of snapping a cigarette end into a small wastebasket from across a room. An art, I believe, of which most male smokers are true masters only when either they don't care a hoot whether or not the butt goes into the basket or the room has been cleared of eyewitnesses, including, quite so to speak, the cigarette snapper himself. I'm going to try hard not to chew on that illustration, delectable as I find it, but I do think it proper to append – to revert momentarily to curb marbles – that after Seymour himself shot a marble, he would be all smiles when he heard a responsive click of glass striking glass, but it never appeared to be clear to him *whose* winning click it was. And it's also a fact that someone almost invariably had to pick up the marble he'd won and *hand* it to him.

Thank God that's over. I can assure you I didn't order it.

I think – I *know* – this is going to be my last 'physical'

notation. Let it be reasonably funny. I'd love to clear the air before I go to bed.

It's an Anecdote, sink me, but I'll let it rip: At about nine, I had the very pleasant notion that I was the Fastest Boy Runner in the World. It's the kind of queer, basically extracurricular conceit, I'm inclined to add, that dies hard, and even today, at a super-sedentary forty, I can picture myself, in *street* clothes, whisking past a series of distinguished but hard-breathing Olympic milers and waving to them, amiably, without a trace of condescension. Anyway, one beautiful spring evening when we were still living over on Riverside Drive, Bessie sent me to the drugstore for a couple of quarts of ice cream. I came out of the building at that very same magical quarter hour described just a few paragraphs back. Equally fatal to the construction of this anecdote, I had sneakers on – sneakers surely being to anyone who happens to be the Fastest Boy Runner in the World almost exactly what red shoes were to Hans Christian Andersen's little girl. Once I was clear of the building, I was Mercury himself, and broke into a 'terrific' sprint up the long block to Broadway. I took the corner at Broadway on one wheel and kept going, doing the impossible: *increasing* speed. The drugstore that sold Louis Sherry ice cream, which was Bessie's adamant choice, was three blocks north, at 113th. About halfway there, I tore past the stationery store where we usually bought our newspapers and magazines, but blindly, without noticing any acquaintances or relatives in the vicinity. Then, about a block farther on, I picked up the sound of pursuit at my rear, plainly conducted on foot. My first, perhaps typically New Yorkese thought was that the cops were after me – the charge, conceivably, Breaking Speed Records on a Non-School-Zone Street. I strained to get a little more speed out of my body, but it was no use. I felt a hand clutch out at me and grab hold of my sweater just where the winning-team numerals should have been, and, good and scared, I broke my speed with the awkwardness of a gooney bird coming to a stop. My pursuer was, of course, Seymour, and he was looking pretty damned scared himself. 'What's the *mat*ter? What *hap*pened?' he asked me frantically. He was still holding on to my sweater. I yanked myself loose from his hand and informed him, in the rather scatological idiom of the neighborhood, which I won't record here verbatim, that *nothing* had happened, *nothing* was the matter, that I was just *running*, for cryin' out loud. His relief was prodigious. 'Boy, did you scare me!' he said. 'Wow, were you moving! I could hardly catch *up* with you!' We then went along, at a walk, to the drugstore together. Perhaps strangely, perhaps not strangely at all, the morale of the now Second-Fastest Boy Runner in the World had not been very perceptibly lowered. For one thing, I had been outrun by *him*. Besides, I was extremely busy noticing that he was panting a lot. It was oddly diverting to see him pant.

I'm finished with this. Or, rather, it's finished with me. Fundamentally, my mind has always balked at any kind of ending. How many stories have I torn up since I was a boy simply because they had what that old Chekhov-baiting noise Somerset Maugham calls a Beginning, a Middle, and an End? Thirty-five? Fifty? One of the thousand reasons I quit going to the theatre when I was about twenty was that I resented like hell filing out of the theatre just because some playwright was forever slamming down his silly curtain. (What ever became of that stalwart bore Fortinbras? Who eventually fixed *his* wagon?) Nonetheless, I'm done here. There are one or two more fragmentary physical-type remarks I'd like to make, but I feel too strongly that my time is *up*. Also, it's twenty to seven, and I have a nine-o'clock class. There's just enough time for a half-hour nap, a shave, and maybe a cool, refreshing blood bath. I have an impulse – more of an old urban reflex than an impulse, thank God – to say something mildly caustic about the twenty-four young ladies, just back from big weekends at Cambridge or Hanover or New Haven, who will be waiting for me in Room 307, but I can't finish writing a description of Seymour – even a bad description, even one where my ego, my perpetual lust to share top billing with him, is all over the place – without being conscious of the good, the real. This is too grand to be said (so I'm just the man to say it), but I can't be my brother's brother for nothing, and I know – not always, but I *know* – there is no single thing I do that is more important than going into that awful Room 307. There isn't one girl in there, including the Terrible

Miss Zabel, who is not as much my sister as Boo Boo or Franny. They may shine with the misinformation of the ages, but they shine. This thought manages to stun me: There's no place I'd really rather go right now than into Room 307. Seymour once said that all we do our whole lives is go from one little piece of Holy Ground to the next. Is he *never* wrong?

Just go to bed, now. Quickly. Quickly and slowly.